the
**short
ish**
project

The Pamela Papers

A Largely
E-pistolary Story of
Academic
Pandemic
Pandemonium

March 2020
The Week before
the Pandemic Shutdown

3/4/2020
Professor Pamela Pankhurst To-Do List

- Make Spring break To-Do List
- Make Shopping List (buy toilet paper!)
- Write Accreditation E-mails
- Go to Third Thursday lunch presentation
- Prep Intro to Creative Writing and Advanced Speechwriting
- Answer student e-mails
- Throw away Clarissa's toothbrush and box up all her gifts
- Eat chocolate and nurse broken heart
- Check out thrillers and romance novels from public library
- Channel surf
- COLLAPSE AND SLEEP FOR A WEEK

The Sanford Liberal Arts College Campus Rag Online, "A Student Newspaper, not a Snoozepaper," March 4 2020

Corrections
Last week, we reported that Mrs. Pamela Pankhurst, who teaches and has an office in Wortz Hall, just received the Columbia Poetry Prize for a book of poems that she wrote and would be traveling to South America to accept her award. We also reported that she speaks fluent Spanish.

Correction: Mrs. Pankhurst does not speak fluent Spanish. We regret the error.

From: Harris, Kaitlyn D.
Thurs 3/04/2020 11:20 AM
To: Pankhurst, Pamela
Subject: Missing Class

Mrs. Pankhurst,

I can't come to class today because I have to rehome my cat and move dorm rooms so please let me know if I'm going to miss anything.

Kaitlyn

From: Pankhurst, Pamela
Thurs 3/04/2020 11:40 AM
To: Harris, Kaitlyn D.
Subject: Missing Class

Dear Kaitlyn,

I'm sorry to hear that you had to rehome your cat. I remember the poems you wrote about her last semester, especially "My Cat Lunges at Birds on the Windowpane," "My Cat Totes around Squawking Robins in the Garden," and "The Bottomless Hunger of My Cat."

But do keep in mind that you've been absent fourteen times and I have an attendance policy.

Dr. Pankhurst

From: Harris, Kaitlyn D.
Thurs 3/04/2020 11:42 AM
To: Pankhurst, Pamela
Subject: Missing Class

Mrs. Pankhurst,

This time is totally not my fault. There was an incident in my dorm involving the untimely and traumatic death of a canary and I'm really freaking out. Just ask Dr. Wilson he'll back me up he's the one who said I have to move.

Kaitlyn

From: Pankhurst, Pamela
Thurs 3/04/2020 11:44 AM
To: Harris, Kaitlyn D.
Subject: Missing Class

Dear Kaitlyn,

I'm so sorry to hear about the death of a bird in your dorm, but I'm not quite sure why this necessitates your missing class. MR. Wilson should feel free to contact me if there's information that I need.

DR. Pankhurst

From: Harris, Kaitlyn D.
Thurs 3/04/2020 11:46 AM
To: Pankhurst, Pamela
Subject: Missing Class

Mrs. Pankhurst,

So what happened is my emotional support cat ate my roommates emotional support canary and I had to rehome my cat and I found an emotional support woolly bear caterpillar but I'm afraid that my roommates new replacement canary is going to mistake my caterpillar for an earthworm and eat it. So that's why I have to miss class and move. Dr. Wilson will send you a note.

Kaitlyn

From: Pankhurst, Pamela
Thurs 3/04/2020 12:00 PM
To: Harris, Kaitlyn D
Subject: Missing Class

Dear Kaitlyn,

Wow. Please keep up with the syllabus.

DR. Pankhurst, PhD

The Sanford Liberal Arts College Campus Rag Online, "A Student Newspaper, not a Snoozepaper," March 4 2020

Amended Corrections
Last week, we reported that Mrs. Pamela Pankhurst, who teaches and has an office in Wortz Hall, just received the Columbia Poetry Prize for a book of poems that she wrote and would be traveling to South America to accept her award. We also reported that she speaks fluent Spanish.

Correction: Mrs. Pankhurst does not speak fluent Spanish. We regret the error.

Additional Correction: Mrs. Pankhurst will not be traveling to South America. We regret the error.

From: The Office of President Elaine J. Moto-Lenovo
Thurs 3/04/2020 12:00 PM
To: Faculty and Staff
Subject: Search for Academic Dean and Vice President of Academic Affairs

Dear Colleagues,

The president's office has made the decision that the search for a new dean and vice president of academic affairs will be confidential. Our determination that this is the best route is based on two factors.

First, we are faced with unusual conditions caused by the increasing threat of the global pandemic. Second, it is imperative that we attract the best possible candidates who may fear repercussions from their home institutions if their job search becomes public.

There will be no public presentations or meetings with constituencies. The committee, whose membership is confidential, hopes to conclude this search by the time of Dean Bill Howard's retirement in April.

Sincerely,

Elaine

From: Pankhurst, Pamela
Thurs 3/04/2020 12:01 PM
To: Raj Patel, Chair of the Division of BESOD
Subject: FWD: Search for Academic Dean and Vice President of Academic Affairs

OMG! I stopped by your office to debrief but I don't guess you were there, since when I listened at the door I didn't hear anyone humming under his breath.

Anyway—whoa! Did you see that e-mail? Somehow despite the glacial pace of academic change, we're going to hire a new dean in six weeks' time? And with what faculty input? And none of us gets to meet the candidates? And they're announcing it right before spring break when half of our colleagues are in the process of leaving town?

From: Raj Patel, Chair of the Division of BESOD
Thurs 3/04/2020 12:10 PM
To: Pankhurst, Pamela
Subject: FWD: Search for Academic Dean and Vice President of Academic Affairs

!!!!???? :(:(:(

Also, I can feel you jiggling your foot manically from all the way across the building, so you have no right to complain about my humming!

The Sanford Liberal Arts College Campus Rag Online, "A Student Newspaper, not a Snoozepaper," March 4 2020

Amended Corrections:
Last week, we reported that Mrs. Pamela Pankhurst, who teaches and has an office in Wortz Hall, just received the Columbia Poetry Prize for a book of poems that she wrote and would be traveling to South America to accept her award. We also reported that she speaks fluent Spanish.

Correction: Mrs. Pankhurst does not speak fluent Spanish. We regret the error.

Additional Correction: Mrs. Pankhurst will not be traveling to South America. We regret the error.

Additional Correction: Mrs. Pankhurst isn't married. It should have been Miss Pankhurst. We regret the error.

From: Brownscar, Bessie
Thurs 3/04/2020 1:30 PM
To: Faculty and Staff
Subject: Today's Third Thursday Presentation

Colleagues,

Just in case you missed today's amazing Third Thursday Presentation by our new colleague Dr. Alma Revers-Arden—and I'm embarrassed that so few of you showed up to support her—I want to share my introduction:

Alma Revers-Arden is a triple threat. She does it all and makes it look effortless: research, service, teaching. An article she wrote appeared last year in one of the leading publications of the Sports Medicine and Exercise field, *The International Journal of Competitive Backward Walking in North America.*

She also serves on fourteen committees, chairing three of them. She's a brilliant teacher: I talked to one of her students who said that her classes are really fun. She elegantly balances a hundred advisees; a course overload; her husband, fellow professor Dr. Bobby Arden; and their two profoundly gifted children while also doing cutting edge research on the Competitive Sideways Walking Movement, tracing its historical and physiological origins in Backward Walking by way of Forward Walking methodologies. . .

From: Raj Patel, Chair of the Division of BESOD
Thurs 3/04/2020 1:44 PM
To: Pankhurst, Pamela
Subject: FWD: Today's Third Thursday Presentation

Did Alma die?

From: Pankhurst, Pamela
Thurs 3/04/2020 2:20 PM
To: Raj Patel, Chair of the Division of BESOD
Subject: FWD: Today's Third Thursday Presentation

Huh? I just got out of class and I don't know what you're talking about.

From: Raj Patel, Chair of the Division of BESOD
Thurs 3/04/2020 2:25 PM
To: Pankhurst, Pamela
Subject: FWD: Today's Third Thursday Presentation

Didn't Bessie Brownscar just send us her obituary?

From: Student Affairs
Thurs 3/04/2020 2:30 PM
To: Faculty and Staff
Subject: Faculty/Student Sleepover Event!

Hey Slackers!

The SLAC student/faculty relations team met last week and voted to promote our student-centered values by creating a new activity to help faculty understand the day-to-day pressures of student life. On Friday, April 3, 2020, they will be sponsoring their first student/faculty sleepover. Select faculty will be invited to spend a night in the dorm with a group of students from their departments. Watch for your invitations!

From: Pankhurst, Pamela
Thurs 3/04/2020 2:40 PM
To: Humanities and Social Sciences Faculty
Subject: Accreditation

Dear Colleagues,

Our accreditation portfolio revision is due by May 1 to the International and National Experiential

School Consortiums and Programs in Education (INESCAPE). As you may know, we failed our first round and now need to scramble to rectify the issues that INESCAPE has identified.

While I have been appointed SLAC's INESCAPE representative, I have no background in education and am only the coordinator. Several of you responded to my request for documentation of the INESCAPE standards last summer by mailing me piles of unmarked syllabi before departing for European vacations and Disney Cruises or turning off your phones to sunbathe in your yards. Here is the first set of standards, which we did not pass (keep in mind that we have several other sets to pass in the coming months as well):

> Document, using syllabi with highlighted relevant statements and annotated sample student work, that your area meets the following standards.
>
> 1.0 Through effective modeling and pedagogy, instructor will:
> 1.1 Help students develop lifelong habits of learning
> 1.2 Ensure that students are engaged citizens
> 1.3 Promote enriching life experiences
> 1.4 Demonstrate habits that encourage diversity and inclusion.

To support Standard 1.1, Bessie had all of her students sign statements that read, "I promise to engage in lifelong learning." The accrediting agency has rejected this as valid supporting evidence.

Here's an example of a problem mentioned by INESCAPE: Buck, I don't think it's clear how your syllabus statement, "In this class, we will subvert the historicality in and between polymorphous and architectonic countermodernities," supports Standard 1.3. Could you elaborate?

You all, I don't want to do this either, and I especially don't want to spend break on this, but we're going to lose our accreditation if you don't take this more seriously. Our deadline to respond to the first set of standards is rapidly approaching.

Best,

Pamela

From: Raj Patel, Chair of the Division of BESOD
Thurs 3/04/2020 4:00 PM
To: Pankhurst, Pamela
Subject: FWD: Faculty/Student Sleepover Event!

All of the hand-holding is bad enough, but now they want us to SLEEP with our students?

From: Student Affairs
Thurs 3/04/2020 4:15 PM
To: Faculty and Staff
Subject: Faculty/Student Sleepover Event!

The student/faculty sleepover has been postponed due to concerns about the global pandemic. We hope to reschedule it for the end of April! Stay tuned!

From: Smith, Lana
Thurs 3/04/2020 4:15 PM
To: Pankhurst, Pamela
Subject: Fall Registration

Hi Professor,

I forgot to come for my advising appointment a couple of weeks ago and if I don't register for fall tonight I can't get into Professor Patel's Economics class or Professor Baker's Business Administration class and I hear they are AWESOME. Can I come by for advising now or could you just take off my advising hold?

Lana

From: Pankhurst, Pamela
Thurs 3/04/2020 4:18 PM
To: Smith, Lana
Subject: Fall Registration

Dear Lana,

Sorry, but I have my night class in a bit. Do you have a tentative schedule you could send me?

Prof. Pankhurst

From: Smith, Lana
Thurs 3/04/2020 4:25 PM
To: Pankhurst, Pamela
Subject: Fall Registration

Hi Professor,

I haven't written it down but I've figured it all out in my head.

Lana
From: Pankhurst, Pamela
Thurs 3/04/2020 4:26 PM
To: Smith, Lana
Subject: Fall Registration

Hi Lana,

Unfortunately, I can't directly access the contents of your brain, so you will have to write down your tentative schedule and send it to me. Also, aren't you an English and writing major? The business administration class is at the same time as the required Intro to Literary Studies.

Prof. Pankhurst

From: Smith, Lana
Thurs 3/04/2020 4:28 PM
To: Pankhurst, Pamela
Subject: Fall Registration

I'm planning to be a famous fantasy novelist, but in case it takes me a few months after graduation to establish myself, I might go to law school. Buck said that business would also be a practical choice.

From: Pankhurst, Pamela
Thurs 3/04/2020 4:29 PM
To: Smith, Lana
Subject: Fall Registration

Writing and literature are excellent foundations for law school and also develop skills that are essential in any workplace. I'd advise you to take a variety of courses.

From: Smith, Lana
Thurs 3/04/2020 4:35 PM
To: Pankhurst, Pamela
Subject: Fall Registration

I don't really care about reading literature except my own. I'm completely original and don't want to be influenced by anyone else.

From: Pankhurst, Pamela
Thurs 3/04/2020 4:37 PM
To: Smith, Lana
Subject: Fall Registration

Well, if you're an English major you do have to take critical theory. I'd also suggest that you read to find out how other writers solve craft problems and discover what is truly original and what's been done before. And it's not a bad idea to develop a range of skills in different genres.

From: Pankhurst, Pamela
Thurs 3/04/2020 4:39 PM
To: Clasp, Elodie
Subject: Student Information for INESCAPE accreditation

Hi Elodie,

Since you are the president of the Future Business Leaders of America Club, I am hoping you can give me some information that will help me to support standards related to civic engagement for our INESCAPE accreditation. To start, I'm wondering if you can give me a list of Humanities and Social Science majors who are involved.

Professor Pankhurst

From: Clasp, Elodie
Thurs 3/04/2020 4:45 PM
To: Pankhurst, Pamela
Subject: Student Information for INESCAPE accreditation

I don't really know. To be honest, the whole thing is total chaos. All anyone ever does is gossip and eat cookies.

From: Pankhurst, Pamela
Thurs 3/04/2020 4:47 PM
To: Clasp, Elodie
Subject: Student Information for INESCAPE accreditation

Does the faculty advisor keep a membership roster? And what is his role in making sure that things run smoothly?

From: Clasp, Elodie
Thurs 3/04/2020 4:49 PM
To: Pankhurst, Pamela
Subject: Student Information for INESCAPE accreditation

Buck doesn't really do anything. He thinks we should figure it out on our own.

From: Pankhurst, Pamela
Thurs 3/04/2020 4:51 PM
To: Clasp, Elodie
Subject: Student Information for INESCAPE accreditation

Maybe you should approach your advisor about your concerns? Also, can you give me more information about the club in general? Goals, officers, mission statement? What resources do we need to make it more educational and rewarding?

From: Clasp, Elodie
Thurs 3/04/2020 4:52 PM
To: Pankhurst, Pamela
Subject: Student Information for INESCAPE accreditation

I don't think Buck would like it if he knew we were talking about him.

From: Pankhurst, Pamela
Thurs 3/04/2020 4:55 PM
To: Clasp, Elodie
Subject: Student Information for INESCAPE accreditation

Hi Elodie,

I'm confused by your last e-mail. We aren't really talking about Buck. We're talking about the club and the information I need for the accreditation portfolio. Buck is aware that I am asking questions related to accreditation, and I could copy him on these e-mails, but the accrediting agency will take more seriously what you say apart from the input of the advisor. I will keep all names confidential.

Professor Pankhurst

From: Clasp, Elodie
Thurs 3/04/2020 4:57 PM
To: Pankhurst, Pamela
Subject: Student Information for INESCAPE accreditation

Buck has told us that if we talk behind his back, he'll find out. He said he has eyes in the back of his head and spies everywhere! We're going to get in trouble!

From: Pankhurst, Pamela
Thurs 3/04/2020 5:00 PM
To: Clasp, Elodie
Subject: Student Information for INESCAPE accreditation

Elodie,

I'm concerned about your last statements. Buck is not omniscient and he can't ask people not to talk about the club. Do you want me to ask him to let you know it's okay to talk about it? I'm happy to take responsibility for raising these questions. I'm a full professor who has been appointed to take charge of our accreditation portfolio, so there are no prohibitions against me discussing this with you. Your name will be kept anonymous, so there is no reason not to talk to me. However, if you want him to give you permission, I can contact him.

Professor Pankhurst

From: Clasp, Elodie
Thurs 3/04/2020 5:05 PM
To: Pankhurst, Pamela
Subject: Student Information for INESCAPE accreditation

Please don't contact Buck! If he finds out, I'll be in so much trouble. If he finds out I've talked to you at all, he'll be really mad.

From: Smith, Lana
Thurs 3/04/2020 5:06 PM
To: Pankhurst, Pamela
Subject: Fall Registration

Dr. Baker says that you can't really do anything with English and Writing and that Business will prepare me for the real world and actually help me get into law school too. Also, I always make As in his classes and I made a C in my last English class, so maybe I'm better at Business. Also, he's a leader in his field.

From: Pankhurst, Pamela
Thurs 3/04/2020 5:08 PM
To: Smith, Lana
Subject: Fall Registration

I think that you'll find that all of your professors have strong credentials in their fields.

From: Pankhurst, Pamela
Thurs 3/04/2020 5:10 PM
To: Raj Patel, Chair of the Division of BESOD
Subject: Argh

Buck Baker is at it again! He has been insufferable ever since he was elected faculty senate president. Now he's poaching another student. I predict she'll bring a change of major form right after spring break.

Also, I just had the weirdest exchange with a student I need to interview about the Future Business Leaders club. I can't even.

AND WHY IS HE THE ADVISOR FOR THE STUDENT NEWSPAPER? He's got no journalism experience whatsoever. I swear, he purposely tries to get them to make mistakes.

And does he think we're impressed by that big book he carries around all the time, *The Dictionary of Multisyllabic Words, Pretentious Phrases, and Impenetrable Academic Jargon* or whatever it's called?

From: Smith, Lana
Thurs 3/04/2020 5:25 PM
To: Pankhurst, Pamela
Subject: Fall Registration

I've decided to change my major to Business. Can I come by now to have you sign the form?

From: Craig, Brittney
Thurs 3/04/2020 5:27 PM
To: Pankhurst, Pamela
Subject: Missing Class

Hey, Prof, I won't be in class today. Rhianne is presenting her story on a tense mother-daughter relationship. It's been really triggering for me ever since my mom and I had a big argument when she told me I couldn't drive her new car to Florida for spring break. Can you believe that she's making me drive her old junker instead?

I'll be in class a week from Tuesday if I make it back from Florida LOL and I'll have copies for everyone of my fantasy story about the brutal massacre of a race of human-like creatures. Have a great break!

The Sanford Liberal Arts College Campus Rag Online, "A Student Newspaper, not a Snoozepaper," March 4 2020

Corrected Corrections:
Last week, we reported that Mrs. Pamela Pankhurst, who teaches and has an office in Wortz Hall, just received the Columbia Poetry Prize for a book of poems that she wrote and would be traveling to South America to accept her award. We also reported that she speaks fluent Spanish.

Correction: Mrs. Pankhurst does not speak fluent Spanish. We regret the error.

Additional Correction: Mrs. Pankhurst will not be traveling to South America. We regret the error.

Additional Correction: Mrs. Pankhurst isn't married. It should have been Miss Pankhurst.

Additional additional correction: Miss Pankhurst actually got the award from some university in New York. We regret the error.

...

March 2020
The Weekend before
the Pandemic Shutdown

3/5/2020
Professor Pamela Pankhurst To-Do List

Spring Break:
- Follow up with agent on proposal for *Grease: A Musical for Senior Citizens*
- Grade 152 student essays
- Groceries (buy toilet paper!)
- Finish accreditation standard 1 and start on 2
- Post picture on Instagram of *Remembrance of Things Past* with caption "What I'm Reading Over Spring Break"
- Finish reading *Random Rash Reckless Love* and *Sacrificial Bones*
- Post on Facebook links to *Helvetica: The Documentary* and *Linotype: The Film* with caption "What I'm Watching Over Spring Break"
- Watch *Dawson's Creek* and *Murder She Wrote*
- Tweet about how Derrida changed my life

- Watch *Beverly Hills 90210*
- Donate Clarissa's clothes and books to Goodwill
- Write angry letter and tear it into little pieces
- SLEEP

From: Computer Technology and Maintenance
Fri 3/05/2020 8:30 AM
To: Faculty
Subject: Technology at Home

If you do not have a desktop at home or an office laptop that can be moved to your home, please report back immediately.

From: Pankhurst, Pamela
Fri 3/05/2020 8:40 AM
To: Raj Patel, Chair of the Division of BESOD
Subject: FWD: Technology at Home

???

From: Dean Howard
Fri 3/05/2020 8:40 AM
To: Pankhurst, Pamela
Subject: Concerns

Pamela,

I had a very concerning conversation with Buck Baker today at six a.m. at the dining hall. One of our top students, Elodie Clasp, had stopped in to see him at midnight—you know what a hard worker he is and what late hours he keeps! She relayed to him that you had initiated an e-mail correspondence with the intent of manipulating her into badmouthing Buck.

Furthermore, she claims that you said, "I'm a full professor and I can do or say whatever I want." Buck claims that you are "incentivizing hypervisibility" and he wants this practice to stop.

Miss Clasp was actually at the dining hall eating breakfast with Buck and she corroborated his account.

Furthermore, she looked very stressed, with mussed hair and clothes askew, and kept yawning as if she had barely slept.

After spring break, we will be required to launch an investigation into your inappropriate conduct in your interactions with students.

Bill

From: Pankhurst, Pamela
Fri 3/05/2020 8:50 AM
To: Dean Howard
Subject: Concerns

Bill,

You've got to be kidding. You dumped this whole accreditation thing on me and now you're threatening to investigate me because I discussed a student club with the student president? That makes no sense

[Saved to Draft Folder]

From: The Office of President Elaine J. Moto-Lenovo
Fri 3/05/2020 8:49 AM
To: Faculty and Staff
Subject: Bill Howard's Retirement

Dear Colleagues,

Due to the increasing threat of the worldwide pandemic, we must all must remain nimble during this unprecedented time! In order to ensure continuity and stability, we will be imminently bringing to a conclusion our search for a new dean and VPAA.

Therefore, Dean Bill Howard has agreed to take early retirement. Today will be Dean Howard's last day. Please extend your appreciation for his twenty years of service to our campus and your warmest wishes for this next stage of his life.

Sincerely,

Elaine

From: Pankhurst, Pamela
Fri 3/05/2020 8:55 AM
To: Raj Patel, Chair of the Division of BESOD
Subject: FWD: Bill Howard's Retirement

???

...

3/8/2020
Professor Pamela Pankhurst Grocery List

- Thirty frozen meals
- Five boxes of pasta
- Five jars of pasta sauce
- Ten boxes of cereal
- Five loaves of bread (freeze four)
- Fifteen bags of frozen vegetables
- Twenty cans of vegetables
- Three pack of ibuprofen
- ~~Hand sanitizer~~
- Extra soap
- ~~Chlorox wipes~~
- Baby wipes?
- ~~50 rolls of toilet paper~~
- ~~One roll of toilet paper~~
- Facial tissues

From: Pankhurst, Pamela
Mon 3/08/2020 10:30 AM
To: Emily Bronty, Gondal Literary Agency
Subject: follow-up: my proposal

Hi Emily,

I am writing to inquire about the status of my proposal for GREASE SR.: A MUSICAL (Alternate Title: ROGAINE). As you may recall, I sent it to you a few weeks ago and am pasting the synopsis below to refresh your memory:

Many popular musicals have been issued in "junior editions" for middle school productions, but what about our senior citizens? There is a dearth of material for dramatic productions in retirement communities, assisted living facilities, nursing homes, and senior activity centers. I propose to fill that gap by recreating a series of musicals specifically directed at senior performers, musicians, producers, and audiences.

GREASE SR. will focus on the romance between Sandy, an Australian widow, and Danny, a retired mechanic who is something of a player among the assisted living community crowd. What happens when Sandy and Danny fall in love in the outpatient waiting room before their colonoscopies—and then discover that Sandy is relocating to the retirement community where Danny has his reputation as a lady's man (actually the only man) to protect?

Danny's a homebody who prefers bowling and Bingo. He's set in his ways and hasn't updated his wardrobe in 30 years. Sandy likes karaoke and travel, loves fashion, is designing her own tattoo, and ziplines and snow tubes. Danny wins her heart by mowing her lawn and bringing her coffee, and by the end, he's even willing to take up daily workouts and invest in better fitting pants. This story shifts from the original GREASE's tensions of young love to the calmer, slower pace of mature love. Songs will include "Maturely Securely Devoted to You," "Alone at the Social Security Office," "It's Raining on Bingo Night," and "Snail-paced Land Yacht."

I look forward to hearing from you.

Best,

Pamela

From: Emily Bronty, Gondal Literary Agency
Mon 3/08/2020 2:30 PM
To: Pankhurst, Pamela
Subject: GREASE SR: A MUSICAL (ALT TITLE ROGAINE)

Hi Pamela,

I did not forget about you! In fact, I'm glad you gave me a little nudge because I was planning to get back to you today with the good news: Broadway Play Publishing Inc. would like to commission your services as librettist and lyricist for GREASE SR.: A MUSICAL (ALT TITLE: ROGAINE) and offer you a contract for three works in your series of senior musicals. I'll call you in a bit to go over the details. Thanks for your patience!

Em

INESCAPE Accreditation Standard #2

2.0 Through effective modeling and pedagogy, the instructor will
    2.1 Help students develop lifelong habits of inhalation and exhalation in basically equal proportions
    2.2 Promote life experiences in the daily lives of students
    2.3 Demonstrate whether humans are

    inherently good or evil
  2.4 Reveal whether an omnipotent god can create a boulder even he/she/they can't lift

From: Pankhurst, Pamela
Mon 3/08/2020 3 PM
To: Raj Patel, Chair of the Division of BESOD; Patel, Saanvi
Subject: Grousing Session

What are you guys doing tonight? I have the most amazing news, and I'm having trouble focusing. I've been trying to work on this accreditation, but my eyes keep crossing and none of the standards make any sense.

From: Patel, Saanvi
Mon 3/08/2020 3:30 PM
To: Pankhurst, Pamela
Subject: Grousing Session

Come on over! I will make you rice with vegetables and no spices for your wimpy American palate! We will celebrate your news and Raj can hum and you can jiggle your foot and we will watch *Jeopardy!* and then find Karaoke versions of Abba on YouTube so we can sing along!

From: The Office of President Elaine J. Moto-Lenovo
Tues 3/09/2020 12:00 PM
To: Faculty and Staff
Subject: Search for Academic Dean and Vice President of Academic Affairs

Dear Colleagues,

We are pleased to announce that, given the current unusual situation, we have been able to track fast the search for an academic dean and VPAA and that Dr. Charlotte Smith Andrews has agreed to immediately assume the position. Please welcome Dr. Andrews!

Sincerely,

Elaine

From: Pankhurst, Pamela
Tues 3/09/2020 12:10 PM
To: Raj Patel, Chair of the Division of BESOD
Subject: FWD: Search for Academic Dean and Vice President of Academic Affairs

What the hell? Track fast? Did Elaine mean *fast track*? Do you have Dr. Andrews's resume? Who is she? Where'd she come from? I can't find her online at all. Not even on Rate My Professor. How does anyone avoid getting rated on Rate my Professor?

From: Raj Patel, Chair of the Division of BESOD
Tues 3/09/2020 12:30 PM
To: Pankhurst, Pamela
Subject: Fwd: Search for Academic Dean and Vice President of Academic Affairs

Buck was on the search committee. He said that all interviews were conducted via Google Hangout and he forwarded me her resume. He said he really liked her. Felt like they spoke the same language. Don't share it with anyone—I think all of the materials were supposed to be top secret.

Resume For Dr. Charlotte Smith Andrews

Work Experience

2019-2020 Research Associate
National Educational Policy Think Tank
Washington D.C.

- Focused on issues designed to transcend heteronormative discourse and institute synecdochic, dialectical, teradactylic, and liminal hegemonies;
- Mediated, elucidated, obfuscated, legitimated, medicated, and retrenched marginalized frameworks;
- Reconciled multiple dichotomies, manifested, predicated on, and redolent of supplanted plant-based problematizations;
- Created multimodal, multi-faceted correlatives to contemporaneously bifurcate and circumvent transgressive paradigms, with a multi-commodal approach to gender parity.

2018-2019 Assistant to the Dead
Monroeville College, Monroeville, PA

- Enforced first lines of communication with division chairs and program directors so as to free up the administrative offices for more substantial matters;
- Accelerated the important work of the university;

- Encouraged review of guidelines so that all could successfully engage in the important cycle of annual review;
- Worked forward to clarify misunderstandings;
- Established policy of grade equity to aid in retention and increase graduation rates;
- Developed consistent motivational messaging in all communications, expressing boundless compassion and urging constituencies to remain energized.

2017-2018
Chair of Arts and Sciences
University of Mauronce

2016-2017
Chair of Department of Academic Studies
University of Imbazilks

Education

Harvard University, 2005
Certificate, *Syllabus Font Selection*

Yale University, 2000
Certificate, *E-mail Responses Using Reply-All: Procedures and Ethics*

Columbiana University, 1995
PhD, Somatic Linguistics
Dissertation: *Obfuscating Language as Mindfulness Practice*

University of California at Barkley, 1994
MFA, Shadow Puppetry

University of Ydyots
BA, Astrobiology and Extraterrestrial Life

From: Pankhurst, Pamela
Tues 3/09/2020 2:00 PM
To: Raj Patel, Chair of the Division of BESOD
Subject: Fwd: Search for Academic Dean and Vice President of Academic Affairs

Given that our administration has been 98 percent male and our faculty is 80 percent male, I'm glad we have a newish female president and that we've hired a female dean. But are there some red flags here? I will admit that I just started skimming after a while, but she's only held her last four positions for a year each? What did she actually DO? And ASSISTANT TO THE DEAD??

From: Raj Patel, Chair of the Division of BESOD
Tues 3/09/2020 2:30 PM
To: Pankhurst, Pamela
Subject: Fwd: Search for Academic Dean and Vice President of Academic Affairs

Oh brother! as you American natives say. I think that "Assistant to the Dead" thing happened because someone scanned her resume into the system—you know how scans screw things up. Or not?

From: The Office of President Elaine J. Moto-Lenovo
Wed 3/10/2020 3:00 PM
To: Faculty and Staff
Subject: Pandemic

Due to the rapid spread of 19 Covid, SLAC is canceling in person classes for the remainder of the semester. Spring break has been extended for an extra week in order to give instructors time to pivot to remote delivery. Instructors should update their syllabi accordingly and submit them to the office of the Dean as soon as possible.

...

March-April 2020
The Weekend before
the Pandemic Shutdown

Professor Pamela Pankhurst To-Do list

- Set up Canvas, Zoom, Box, Google Docs, class e-mail lists
- Practice positioning the computer for maximum flattering Zoom angle
- Practice doing hair and decorating head (earrings, headbands, braids, spitcurls) for maximum flattering Zoom appearance
- Buy more sweatpants
- ~~Find toilet paper!~~
- Move self-help books and YA novels, replace with Western classics, global contemporary literary fiction, and literary criticism for Zoom background
- ~~Rewrite all syllabi and assignments for remote delivery~~
- ~~Teach Classes on Zoom~~

- Rewrite all syllabi and assignments for completely online access
- Switch classes to asynchronous format
- ~~Set up Zoom presentations~~
- Have students write papers in lieu of presentations
- ~~Grade final projects~~
- Fill out forms for Incomplete Grades
- Cancel Cayman Island plane tickets (mine and Clarissa's)
- Stalk Clarissa on Facebook and Instagram
- Lie on couch and stare at ceiling
- Consider the passage of time and the movement of shadows
- Fend off existential crisis

From: Raj Patel, Chair of the Division of BESOD
Tues 3/16/2020 2:30 PM
To: Pankhurst, Pamela
Subject: Today's Training

Did you get a good look at the new dean at the Zoom meeting today? I couldn't see her face. She was sitting in front of that window and her face was a cloud hovering in the midst of a dazzling beam of sunshine.

From: Pankhurst, Pamela
Tues 3/16/2020 3:00 PM
To: Raj Patel, Chair of the Division of BESOD
Subject: Today's Training

I know! Her head looked oddly, perfectly symmetrical, but that's all I could really see. Weird.

She seemed very calm and authoritative, though, don't you think? I liked her voice. It reminded me a bit of Clarissa's. She could be sort of emotionless and terrified of intimacy, though. Sorry. Getting sidetracked here.

...

May 2020
Professor Pamela Pankhurst To-Do List

- Track down remaining students who didn't complete work
- Mark incomplete work
- ~~Buy toilet paper~~
- Dress in cat costume to take out trash to see if neighbors notice
- ~~Learn all of the languages on Duolinguo~~
- Take jiujitsu lessons on YouTube and practice on porch
- Put on soap operas, mute the sound, and invent dialogue
- Organize Tupperware
- Watch body swap/age swap/soul transfer movies on Netflix and Hulu
- Read the novelizations for body swap movies on Netflix and Hulu
- Attend weekly meetings on preparing for the fall semester
- Attend biweekly meetings on pandemic mitigation and guidelines for accessing campus buildings

- Drop a casual note to Clarissa in response to her apology? Or make her suffer for a while?
- Apply for INESCAPE deadline postponement
- Follow up with students who disappear from Zoom conferences
- Consider the nature of impermanence and mortality

From: Charlotte Smith Andrews, VPAA
Mon 5/18/2020 1:00 AM
To: SLAC Faculty
Subject: Pandemic Course Prep

Dear Faculty,

In the Fall, we will be adopting what I have named the SLAC Hy Flex Turnonadime Vacillating ZigZag Seesaw Method of Course Delivery, hereafter referred to as the HFTVXSMCD. Our watchwords will be Adaptability. Elasticity. Fluidity. Changeability. Versatility. Pliability, Variability (AEFCVPV). In other words: faculty should be prepared to be all things to all people.

Do keep in mind that students may choose how they wish to engage in their coursework. They may elect to attend in person, remotely, fully online, and any combination of these or none at all. They may choose to engage by disengaging, they may wish to spread across several classrooms for the sake of social distancing and you will need to figure out how to be in all of the rooms at once, they may choose to engage in nature, in the woods, on the trail, from other states, with or without stable technology, with or without cameras or mics, with or without quizzes, papers, or class discussions. By Friday, May 22, please submit a 30-page single-spaced plan detailing how you will accommodate each of these scenarios.

Please also be sure to record all of your lectures and caption everything that you record. Remember that due to privacy concerns, you must blur the faces and scramble the voices of any students who appear in your recordings. If you have privacy concerns of your own, you may apply for permission to blur your own face and scramble your own voice.

To accommodate all learning styles, please post recorded remarks for auditory learners as well as videotaped versions for visual/auditory learners. In addition, you will need to set your recorded lectures to familiar tunes for musical learners, translate them to algebra for logical and mathematical learners, and create scratch and sniff versions for sensory learners.

Please immediately send your chair a message with information about the instructional modalities that you prefer so that that information can be communicated to students, who may choose alternate instructional modalities instead. We have three months to make this crucial transition. If you work steadily for ninety hours each week over the summer, I believe that you will be fully prepared. You got this!

Remain energized!

With boundless compassion for all of humanity,

Charlotte

...

June 2020
Professor Pamela Pankhurst To-Do List

- ~~Mark incomplete work~~
- Track down students who haven't completed incompletes
- E-mail fall students about online course delivery
- Buy toilet paper!
- Watch news obsessively
- Mail donation to Black Lives Matter
- Send e-mails to students about George Floyd/Breanna Taylor murders
- Request that SLAC administration make statement regarding racial injustice
- Buy more masks
- Dress in evening gown to take out trash to see if neighbors notice
- Take YouTube saxophone lessons
- Look at pictures of puppies and kittens
- Build replica of childhood home with Legos
- Watch movies about amnesia on Netflix and Hulu
- Reorganize spice rack alphabetically
- Figure out where Roomba disappeared to—under couch? Under hutch?

- Do not call or write to check on how Clarissa is doing
- Attend weekly meetings on preparing for the fall semester
- Attend biweekly meetings on pandemic mitigation and guidelines for accessing campus buildings
- Attend training for new teaching platform, Whiplash
- Get some cream to sharpen up borders between face and neck so I don't look so old on Zoom!

From: Pankhurst, Pamela
Thurs 6/04/2020 2:00 PM
To: Charlotte Smith Andrews, VPAA
CC: The Office of President Elaine J. Moto-Lenovo
Subject: Statement regarding racial injustice

Dear Dean Smith Andrews,

Welcome to campus. What a difficult time to take a new job—I hope that you have been settling in. We are all looking forward to meeting you in person.

I'm writing to you because I'm concerned about the many anguished and angry posts I've seen from our students of color on social media in the wake of the murders of George Floyd and Breonna Taylor. I know that many universities have released statements to make their support of their students clear and to enumerate the things that we all need to do better. I have attached a few such statements. Are we planning to make one as a campus? I'm copying in President Moto-Lenovo because I think this is an important issue.

Thanks—

Pamela

From: Charlotte Smith Andrews, VPAA
Fri 6/05/2020 2:00 AM
To: Pankhurst, Pamela
Subject: Statement Regarding Racial Injustice

Dear Pamela,

Thank you for lifting up this very important matter. I bring 30 years of experience with these issues to SLAC and will be forwarding multiple initiatives regarding diversity awareness and training, concentrating on workplace gamification, microlearning, and anti-racism seminars with a particular focus on combatting reverse racism and antiwhite speech. I look forward to proceeding with this important work together.

Remain energized!

With boundless compassion for all of humanity,

Charlotte

From: Pankhurst, Pamela
Fri 6/05/2020 10:00 AM
To: Raj Patel, Chair of the Division of BESOD
Subject: FWD: Statement regarding racial injustice

??????

...

July 2020
Professor Pamela Pankhurst To-Do List

- Track down incomplete work from students who have disappeared
- Dress in academic regalia to take out trash to see if neighbors notice
- Take tap dancing lessons on YouTube and practice on front porch
- Practice jiujitsu on porch
- Invent tap-jiujitsu hybrid moves
- Watch movies about time loops on Netflix and Hulu
- Do not call or write to Clarissa no matter how much she pleads!
- Attend advanced training for Whiplash
- Attend 42,000 Zoom meetings about pandemic measures and curriculum design
- Develop plans for multiple possible "student engagement" scenarios
- Do not work past 7 p.m.!
- GET BACK TO CREATIVE WORK AND ASSESSMENT

...

August 2020
Professor Pamela Pankhurst To-Do List

- Bake Cake resembling roll of toilet paper for Sannvi's birthday
-   (leave on porch for no-contact celebration)
- Go to Walmart at 7 a.m. daily to look for hand sanitizer
- Dress in tutu to take out trash to see if neighbors notice
- Go to more trainings for Whiplash
- Redesign classes for the millionth time
- Set up classes on Whiplash to be prepared to start two weeks early
- Revise classes on Whiplash to accommodate social vs. solitary learners
- ~~Turn in grades for Spring incompletes~~
- Order grocery pickup from Walmart (tell them NOT to substitute chili peppers for garlic, napkins for toilet paper, an orchid for a fruit basket, or a 22 lb bag of wheat flour for loaf of bread!)
- Watch all movies and documentaries on wilderness survival on Netflix and Hulu
- Sign up for Zoom white belt Jiujitsu test
- Write brief note to Clarissa? Maybe just a text?
- GET BACK TO CREATIVE WORK AND ASSESSMENT!!! (work on song lyrics and gather evidence for next assessment standard)
- Pretend that internet failed when tired of Zoom meetings

Grease, Sr.
Alternate Title: *Rogaine*
Sandra Dee, Sr.
(To the Tune of "Look at Me, I'm Sandra Dee")

Look at me, I'm Sandra Dee

Fresh from my colonoscopy

Can't light my fuse till I've had my prune juice

I can't, I'm Sandra Dee.

...

September 2020
Professor Pamela Pankhurst To-Do List

- Take breaks from computer for lunch and dinner!
- Don't eat over computer. It gets crumbs in the keyboard.
- Track down spring students with incompletes
- Read assignments
- Prepare lecture scripts, using iPad as teleprompter
- Record, caption, and upload lectures
- Prepare, record, and caption discussions
- Blur out student faces and scramble voices
- Prepare and upload writing assignments
- Grade discussion boards
- Record points for participation
- Mark peer reviews

- Buy more eye drops
- Buy blue light glasses
- Revise week's assignments on Whiplash
- Jiujitsu white belt Zoom ceremony
- WAIT TWO WEEKS TO RESPOND TO CLARISSA'S TEXT
- TAKE BREAKS. Watch movies about alternate history/urban fantasy/AI
- Don't forget to put on pants before teaching class or taking out trash
- Stare blankly into space at the end of the day

From: Charlotte Smith Andrews, VPAA
Wed 9/09/2020 1:00 AM
To: Faculty
CC: The Office of President Elaine J. Moto-Lenovo
Subject: Substitutions

Dear Faculty,

It has come to my attention that for the last thirty years, our faculty has engaged in sloppy practices that could someday threaten our accreditation should an accrediting officer take note. The fact that no accreditor has raised a single question about this in the past is not an adequate excuse! The number of substitution and directed study forms being submitted for graduating students reflects appalling mismanagement and is unacceptable. Substituting one class for another in a student's program should only be reserved for the most extreme circumstances.

A situation in which many students need your lower-level class and only one needs your upper-level class is not an adequate rationale for allowing the upper-level student to earn credit by taking the lower-level class while assuming a leadership role and completing extra, more challenging, assignments. Nor is it allowable to add a directed study to satisfy this student's requirements. You will need to find a way to offer the required class to the student in question, even if it means that you will have to teach more than four classes in a semester or redesign your program to omit upper-level courses.

Do be aware that we will no longer be allowing overloads or overload pay, that we need at least fifteen students to run any given class, and that we cannot be accredited without offering a robust roster of upper-level courses, however.

Remain energized!

Charlotte

From: The Office of President Elaine J. Moto-Lenovo
Wed 9/09/2020 2:00 PM
To: Faculty
CC: Charlotte Smith Andrews, VPAA
Subject: Substitutions

Faculty,

Please desist and cease from this egregious practice of overusing substitutions and directed studies. Not cool, guys.

Elaine

From: Charlotte Smith Andrews, VPAA
Thurs 9/10/2020 2:00 AM
To: Faculty
CC: The Office of President Elaine J. Moto-Lenovo
Subject: Dr. Brownscar

Dear Faculty,

I'm pleased to inform you that Dr. Bessie Brownscar will be leaving us for other exciting opportunities in the academic enterprise.

Remain energized!

Charlotte

From: Raj Patel, Chair of the Division of BESOD
Thurs 9/10/2020 11:00 AM
To: Pankhurst, Pamela
Subject: FWD: Dr. Brownscar

You do know why Bessie's leaving, right? To graduate, one of her students needed a one credit lifeguarding PE class that could not be held due to the pandemic. The entire curriculum of the lifeguarding class is about obtaining Red Cross certification. So Bessie had the student complete Red Cross certification instead. Same thing, right? Then Bessie applied for a waiver—no PE requirement since the student had fulfilled an equivalent requirement. Makes perfect sense, right?

But Charlotte denied the substitution, saying that Bessie was engaging in duplicitous practices and should be fired for her incompetence. Bessie was so upset she resigned on the spot. I can't even.

The massacre is only beginning.

From: Pankhurst, Pamela
Thurs 9/10/2020 11:30 AM
To: Raj Patel, Chair of the Division of BESOD
Subject: FWD: Dr. Brownscar

OMG. I have to submit substitution paperwork or one of my students will not be able to graduate. Can't wait.

From: Pankhurst, Pamela
Thurs 9/10/2020 12:00 PM
To: Charlotte Smith Andrews, VPAA
CC: W. Ways, Chair of Humanities and Social Sciences
Subject: Substitution waivers for Maria Ruiz

Dear Dr. Smith Andrews,

I must throw myself on your mercy since I will be submitting to you a slew of substitution paperwork for student Maria Ruiz, who is due to graduate in May. After the deaths of both of her parents and two siblings in a horrific fire three years ago, Maria, then a sociology major, published her first novel, which received a *Publisher's Weekly* starred review, raves from the *New York Times* and the *Los Angeles Review of Books*, and the Pen-America First Novel Award. She was invited to teach at the University of Iowa, the world's oldest and most reputable MFA in writing program, beginning next fall provided that she finish a BA degree in creative writing first, the opportunity of a lifetime!

We decided to fast-track Maria through the writing major, skipping core courses like Intro to Fiction and instead giving her core credits for seven advanced courses, which she has taken over the last three semesters. If she does not finish her degree in the next semester, the job at Iowa will no longer be available. If she does graduate from SLAC and immediately obtains this prestigious position, however, we will be able to attract more students by publicizing her successes. This seems to me a win-win for all concerned.

Maria's story is one of tragedy and triumph, of prevailing against all odds. Her success will bring national attention to our program. I hope you will take these unusual circumstances into consideration when you receive Maria's substitution forms.

Pamela

From: W. Ways, Chair of Humanities and Social Sciences
Mon 9/14/2020 7 AM
To: Pankhurst, Pamela
Subject: Substitution waivers for Maria Ruiz

Pamela,

The dean has informed me that she cannot in good conscience support these substitution waivers.

Wily

From: Pankhurst, Pamela
Mon 9/14/2020 9:00 AM
To: Charlotte Smith Andrews, VPAA
CC: W. Ways, Chair of Humanities and Social Sciences
Subject: Substitution waivers for Maria Ruiz

Dear Dr. Smith Andrews,

I am appealing to you to reconsider Maria Ruiz's substitutions. Her tragic story and remarkable accomplishments aside, I must point out that making a plan by which she could complete the English and writing major in three semesters was in keeping with the practices of the previous administration. It was also in line with the revised major that I proposed two years ago and that has been approved at every level on this campus. That major has been in limbo for months, awaiting final approval from the president's office.

Maria should not be penalized for this delay.

Pamela

From: Charlotte Smith Andrews, VPAA
Tues 9/15/2020 12:30 AM
To: Pankhurst, Pamela
CC: W. Ways, Chair of Humanities and Social Sciences
Subject: Substitution waivers for Maria Ruiz

I want to acknowledge that I have read your email albeit past midnight!

Let's find a way to make this a degree that the students will embrace. The classes are for which semesters? This spring, next fall...? Not all directed studies...

Let's talk soon!

Remain energized!

Charlotte

From: Pankhurst, Pamela
Tues 9/15/2020 9:00 AM
To: Charlotte Smith Andrews, VPAA
CC: W. Ways, Chair of Humanities and Social Sciences
Subject: Substitution waivers for Maria Ruiz

Dear Dr. Smith Andrews,

I am not submitting any directed study requests. The substitution forms are for courses that Maria has already taken. As I explained earlier, she has to graduate this spring in order to take the job at Iowa.

I would certainly like to make this a degree that students will embrace. That's why I worked for seven years on the proposal that is currently waiting for final approval. I will send your admin a meeting request.

Best,

Pamela

From: Pankhurst, Pamela
Tues 9/15/2020 9:20 AM
To: Millhouse, Kinsey
Subject: Meeting Request

Hi Kinsey,

Dr. Smith Andrews suggested that we set a Zoom meeting for next week to discuss Maria Ruiz's substitution forms as well as the curriculum of the English and writing program.

Thanks—

Pamela

From: Millhouse, Kinsey
Tues 9/15/2020 9:30 AM
To: Pankhurst, Pamela
Subject: Meeting Request

Pamela,

Dr. Andrews has availability next Tuesday at 9 p.m.

Kinsey

From: W. Ways, Chair of Humanities and Social Sciences
Wed 9/16/2020 7:00 AM
To: Pankhurst, Pamela
Subject: Substitution waivers for Maria Ruiz

Pamela,

The dean has informed me that she will take another look at the submitted paperwork for your student provided that you prepare a minimum 30-page single-spaced document including a rationale for each course substitution, syllabi for the lower-level classes that the student would have taken if they had been offered, syllabi for the upper-level classes that the student took instead, as well as samples of her written work and that of other students in those classes, a complete biography and timeline for the student, copies of professional and customer reviews of her novel, photocopies of the award certificates her novel has won, fan mail from readers across America, and performance comparisons between her and other students as well as a cross-section of Pulitzer-prize-winning authors broken down into pie charts, bar graphs, line graphs, Venn diagrams, and pictograms for easy digestion of your data. The dean asks that you also cut and paste relevant passages regarding major requirements from the course catalogue and alternate requirements from the new major proposal.

Wily

From: Pankhurst, Pamela
Thurs 9/16/2020 2:30 PM
To: Charlotte Smith Andrews VPAA
Subject: Substitution waivers for Maria Ruiz

Dear Dr. Smith Andrews,

Attached please find a list of courses that Maria has taken and a list of core courses I propose substituting them for. I have also enclosed a 30-page single spaced document including:

- a rationale for each course substitution
- syllabi for the lower-level classes that the student would have taken if they had been offered
- syllabi for the upper-level classes that the student took instead
- samples of her written work and that of other students in those classes
- a complete biography and timeline for the student
- copies of professional and customer reviews of her novel
- photocopies of the award certificates her novel has won
- fan mail from readers across America
- performance comparisons between the student and other students
- performance comparisons between the student and a cross-section of Pulitzer-prize-winning authors broken down into pie charts, bar graphs, and line graphs
- relevant passages regarding major requirements from the course catalogue
- and alternate requirements from the new major proposal.

I regret that I am unable to provide Venn diagrams since these are outside of my academic expertise and pictograms since these are beyond my artistic ability. Nevertheless, I think you will see that Maria has met all learning objectives and exceeded all expectations for academic quality and integrity.

Pamela

From: Charlotte Smith Andrews VPAA
Thurs 9/16/2020 11:40 PM
To: Pankhurst, Pamela
Subject: Substitution waivers for Maria Ruiz

Will the classes for which you are requesting substitutions be taught in Spring 2021 or were they taught in Fall 2020?

Keep in mind that offering coursework through directed studies is not a sound educational practice.

Remain energized!

Charlotte

From: Pankhurst, Pamela
Thurs 9/16/2020 11:45 PM
To: Charlotte Smith Andrews VPAA
Subject: Substitution waivers for Maria Ruiz

ALL INFORMATION I HAVE SUBMITTED IS FOR CLASSES TAUGHT IN FALL 2019, SPRING 2020, AND FALL 2020. I WOULD NOT HAVE BEEN ABLE TO SUBMIT WRITING SAMPLES FOR COURSES NOT YET TAUGHT.

Sorry, not yelling. My caps lock was temporarily stuck.

Please note: I am not asking for any directed studies. I am only asking that the courses Maria has taken the last two years count toward her graduate requirements. **Otherwise there is no way that she can graduate.**

Sorry, not screaming. My bold font was temporarily stuck.

Pamela

From: Charlotte Smith Andrews VPAA
Mon 9/20/2020 11:55 PM
To: Pankhurst, Pamela
Subject: Substitution waivers for Maria Ruiz

Pamela,

After a thorough review of your submitted materials, I have approved all paperwork for Maria Ruiz. Let's hold off on our meeting to discuss the writing major until next month. Please schedule a new time with Kinsey Millhouse.
Remain energized!

Charlotte

From: Charlotte Smith Andrews VPAA
Wed 9/22/2020 12:01 AM
To: Students
CC: Faculty
Subject: Concerns

Dear Students,

I want to urge you to take time for self-care as you balance the heavy lifts and deep dives of your coursework. From establishing policies of grade equity to making sure that no one fails as well as a ban on attendance policies, participation requirements, and student learning outcomes that require exertion or undue pressure, I have shown myself to be firmly in your corner.

YOU are the reason for our existence, and if there's anything I can do to enhance your educational experience, please know that I support you. Contact my administrative assistant Kinsey Millhouse should you need to meet with me for any reason. I am here to help YOU!

Remain energized!

With boundless compassion for all of humanity,

Vice President Smith Andrews

...

October 2020
Professor Pamela Pankhurst To-Do List

- Read
- Prepare
- Teach
- Grade
- Read
- Prepare
- Teach
- Grade
- Paperwork
- Conferences

- Buy fish oil for dry eye
- Make doctor appointment
- Request anxiety meds
- Meetings, meetings, meetings
- Knock off at 8 p.m. and TAKE A BREAK
- Practice jiujitsu on porch
- Watch movies about twins separated at birth and TV shows about babies switched at birth
- Like Clarissa's Facebook status?

From: Charlotte Smith Andrews VPAA
Thurs 10/1/2020 12:30 AM
To: Faculty
CC: The Office of President Elaine J. Moto-Lenovo
Subject: Concerns

Dear Faculty,

I have been deluged by students expressing concerns. Fielding their concerns is your job, not mine. Please be sure that you are doing your job, including providing satisfactory and inclusive learning experiences that center the needs and promote the voices of all of your students and anticipate and head off grievances.

Several students have contacted me because professors have been calling on them when they attend Zoom classes without turning on their cameras. Please note that compelling students to turn on cameras or mics is a violation of their privacy and that you need to cease this practice or face disciplinary action.

Remain energized!

With boundless compassion for all of humanity,

Charlotte

From: Charlotte Smith Andrews, VPAA
Fri 10/2/2020 1:30 AM
To: Faculty, School of Humanities and Social Sciences
Subject: Chair Election

Dear Humanities and Social Sciences Faculty,

It is time to elect a new chair of your unit. Attached please find a list of the eight tenured faculty members eligible for this position. Please nominate a candidate by 10/3/2020 at 8:00 a.m.

Remain energized!

Charlotte

From: Maus, Ralph S.
Fri 10/2/2020 9:00 AM
To: Charlotte Smith Andrews, VPAA
CC: Faculty, School of Humanities and Social Sciences
Subject: Chair Election

I do not wish to be considered for the chair position.

From: Zuckerman, Wilbur
Fri 10/2/2020 9:15 AM
To: Charlotte Smith Andrews, VPAA
CC: Faculty, School of Humanities and Social Sciences
Subject: Chair Election

Nobody nominate me. I don't want it.

From: Abubakar, Obi
Fri 10/2/2020 9:20 AM
To: Charlotte Smith Andrews, VPAA
CC: Faculty, School of Humanities and Social Sciences
Subject: Chair Election

I'm already overloaded serving as the "diversity" representative on every committee. Do not nominate me for yet more thankless work.

From: Sagal, Jonathan L.
Fri 10/2/2020 9:30 AM
To: Charlotte Smith Andrews, VPAA
CC: Faculty, School of Humanities and Social Sciences
Subject: Chair Election

I will be unable to entertain a nomination at this time.

From: Kim, Jeo-Yun
Fri 10/2/2020 9:35 AM
To: Charlotte Smith Andrews, VPAA
CC: Faculty, School of Humanities and Social Sciences
Subject: Chair Election

What Obi said. No. Just no.

From: Kotzwinkle, Walter
Fri 10/2/2020 9:45 AM
To: Charlotte Smith Andrews, VPAA
CC: Faculty, School of Humanities and Social Sciences
Subject: Chair Election

Not it!

From: Pankhurst, Pamela
Fri 10/2/2020 2:30 PM
To: Charlotte Smith Andrews, VPAA
CC: Faculty, School of Humanities and Social Sciences
Subject: Chair Election

Dear Charlotte,

Given the responses of Walter, Jonathan, Obi, Wilbur, Jeo-Yun, and Ralph, it seems that there is reluctance to take on the chair position due to the minimal amount of compensation and constantly increasing workload, especially under the stressful conditions of the pandemic. Might a conversation about this with you be fruitful before we put forth nominations?

Best,

Pamela

From: Charlotte Smith Andrews, VPAA
Sun 10/4/2020 1:30 AM
CC: Faculty, School of Humanities and Social Sciences
Subject: Chair Election

Dear Humanities and Social Sciences Faculty,

You have missed the deadline for submitting your nominations. I will need a slate of nominations immediately.

Remain energized!

Charlotte

From: Revers-Arden, Alma
Mon 10/5/2020 8:00 AM
To: Pankhurst, Pamela
Subject: FWD: Chair Election

Hey Pamela,

Are you thinking about running for chair of your unit? I'm thinking of running for chair of mine. I feel like we are so backward, and that I could do something about that.

Alma

From: Pankhurst, Pamela
Mon 10/5/2020 10:00 AM
To: Revers-Arden, Alma
Subject: FWD: Chair Election

Hi Alma,

Well, no one else is willing to do it but Wily, and he's been chair for a gazillion years. I'm worried about time if I take it on, since I have two book contracts and a pending contract to develop a series of musicals. As long as I can keep my research/scholarship course release, a one course reduction that was awarded to me after I published my first nine books and got a job offer from Oxford, I can imagine taking this on, but what are the chances?

I did ask Charlotte for a meeting, but she hasn't responded.

Pamela

From: Charlotte Smith Andrews, VPAA
Mon 10/5/2020 11:35 PM
To: Faculty, School of Humanities and Social Sciences
Subject: Chair Election

The nominations are complete, and the division has selected one candidate, Professor Ways. Please select the candidate that you wish to be the next chair of the division.

Remain energized!

Charlotte

From: Pankhurst, Pamela
Tues 10/6/2020 9:15 AM
To: Charlotte Smith Andrews, VPAA
CC: Faculty, School of Humanities and Social Sciences
Subject: Chair Election

Dear Dr. Smith Andrews,

I'm confused. I asked for a meeting to discuss this position so I could decide whether or not I was willing to be nominated, and I never got a response.
Best,

Pamela

From: Charlotte Smith Andrews, VPAA
Tues 10/6/2020 10:00 AM
To: Pankhurst, Pamela
CC: Faculty, School of Humanities and Social Sciences
Subject: Chair Election

The slate of eligible nominees (tenured faculty) included your name and the eight eligible nominees (Maus, Zuckerman, Abubakar, Kotzwinkle, Sagal, Kim, Pankhurst, Ways) were advanced for selection. Eligible nominees needed to have at least one vote to be placed on the ballot. Only Ways received the vote(s) necessary to be on the election slate. I regret to say that you did not have the support of your division to go forward with a nomination.

Remain energized!

Charlotte

From: Pankhurst, Pamela
Tues 10/6/2020 10:30 AM
To: Charlotte Smith Andrews, VPAA
CC: Faculty, School of Humanities and Social Sciences
Subject: Chair Election

Dr. Smith Andrews,

~~It's not like this is a popularity contest or like there's some high bar to be met in order to receive a nomination. I could have nominated myself, and I didn't, because I wanted to meet with you first!~~

On behalf of the voting members of the Humanities

and Social Sciences, I am writing to respectfully request that the election of a new chair be postponed until we have had sufficient time to discuss our concerns with you.

We're confused about the rushed nature of this process, with considerable confusion about eligibility according to established guidelines that say that no one may hold the chair position for more than two three-year terms, a candidate who has held the position for forty years nominating himself, and one potential candidate denied the opportunity to seek clarification before the ballot was created. I would like to request a more transparent process and clarification of the expectations and role of the chair under our new administration before we go forward with this election.

Respectfully,

Pamela

From: Millhouse, Kinsey
Tues 10/6/2020 3:00 PM
To: Pankhurst, Pamela
Subject: Chair Election

Vice President Andrews has asked me to schedule a meeting with you for tomorrow. She has a five-minute time slot available at noon.

From: Pankhurst, Pamela
Tues 10/6/2020 3:05 PM
To: Raj Patel, Chair of the Division of BESOD
Subject: Chair Election

OMG, I asked for a meeting for tomorrow and she is only giving me five minutes!

From: Raj Patel, Chair of the Division of BESOD
Tues 10/6/2020 3:10 PM
To: Pankhurst, Pamela
Subject: Chair Election

Don't sweat it, as you American natives say. She never keeps track of time.

From: Pankhurst, Pamela
Thurs 10/8/2020 2:30 PM
To: Raj Patel, Chair of the Division of BESOD
Subject: Chair Election

So I met on Zoom with Charlotte. The meeting actually only took five minutes! I just said, "I know this might be a deal breaker, but several years ago I negotiated a course release in exchange for my continued productivity and agreement to use my work to promote our campus nationally and internationally. I would need to keep this release, so as chair, I would only be able to teach one course."

She seemed kind of distracted and impatient and brusque, and said, "I don't know anything about that, but if that's the case, you'd teach one class."

I was taken by surprise. "Well, in that case, I'm okay with running," I said.

"So you will run for chair of your division?" she said, and though her face is always either obscured by light or in shadows (someone needs to talk to her about better lighting/positioning for her Zoom calls!), her head tipped like she was glancing at her watch.

"I guess so. That was surprisingly easy," I said.

"Will that be all?" she asked in that weird expressionless tone she takes on sometimes.

I confirmed that it was, and afterward I told my unit that if they reached a unanimous agreement that they wanted me to do it, I would. So we met, everyone else who was eligible removed their names from consideration, and a ballot came out with me as the only candidate.

From: Raj Patel, Chair of the Division of BESOD
Thurs 10/8/2020 3:00 PM
To: Pankhurst, Pamela
Subject: Chair Election

We will pass notes during chair meetings deciding which fallen celebrities our colleagues resemble (don't you think Buck looks like Harvey Weinstein?). I will hum under my breath and you will jiggle your foot under the table! We will spend Friday evenings eating bland food and grousing about all of the ridiculous expectations. Can't wait!

From: Pankhurst, Pamela
Fri 10/9/2020 10:00 AM
To: Harris, Kaitlyn D.
Subject: Your Poems

Attached please find your marked up poems about your caterpillar, Fuzzy Izzy, "My Caterpillar Gnaws Clover," "Fuzzy Izzy's Yummy Dandelion," and "The Bottomless Hunger of My Caterpillar." I enjoyed the attached photographs—Fuzzy Izzy looks just like a little stuffed animal. But if you want to show him off on Bring Your Pets to Zoom Class Day, you'll have to turn on your camera, since we just kind of had to take your word for it that the sound we were hearing was him chewing on a sunflower.

Grease, Sr.
Alternate Title: *Rogaine*
Routine Procedure
(To the Tune of "Summer Lovin")

(Sandy and Danny together:)

Routine Procedure, prep really sucked

Routine procedure, in the waiting room stuck

(Danny:)

Met a gal crazy for me

(Sandy:)

Met a geezer, cute as could be

(Together:)

Waiting room, love started to bloom

And oh oh that anesthesia

From: HP
Sun 10/11/2020 9:00 PM
To: Pankhurst, Pamela
Subject: Late assignment

Mrs. Pankhurst,

I can't upload my poem on Whiplash because it was due yesterday and I was having internet problems, so I'm attaching it to this e-mail. It's about how much I love hamburgers. Could you give me some feedback before class?

From: Pankhurst, Pamela
Mon 10/12/2020 9:00 AM
To: HP
Subject: Late assignment

Dear Mystery Student,

Who are you?

Dr. Pankhurst

From: HP
Mon 10/12/2020 5:00 PM
To: Pankhurst, Pamela
Subject: Late assignment

It's Harry Porter, you know, in your class? You told us not to write poems that rhyme, but I was kind of proud of my rhymes, like "enjoyed" and "steroid" and "burger" and "no sugar" and "ketchup" and "what's up?" You also said that it's impossible to write a poem that's not about death but I did it!

From: Pankhurst, Pamela
Mon 10/12/2020 5:30 PM
To: HP
Subject: Late assignment

~~I think what I said is that underlying all GOOD poetry is awareness of mortality~~

I think the cows would disagree.

Dr. Pankhurst

...

November 2020
Professor Pamela Pankhurst To-Do List

- Read
- Prepare
- Teach
- Grade
- Read
- Prepare
- Teach
- Grade
- Paperwork
- Conferences
- Meet with Dean about program revisions
- Respond (casually) to Clarissa's e-mail
- Work on "We Go Together" (incorporate chorus of socks that sing as they're paired off?)
- Work on third accreditation standard

- Study for jiujitsu blue belt (will go better with my outfits, even if no one can see them on Zoom)

Inescape Accreditation Standard 3

3.1 The program prepares the candidate with knowledge, understanding, and regular practices that enable the candidates to
3.1.1 Use walking or some equivalent as a major form of ambulation
3.1.2. Use chewing as a primary form of mastication
3.1.3 Include effective swallowing procedures in his/her/their repertoire of pre-digestive habits
3.1.4 Demonstrate through regular practice how inhaling and exhaling are interrelated
3.1.5. Integrate breathing, eating, and sleeping in his/her/their daily life-sustaining methodology.

From: Pankhurst, Pamela
Tues 11/3/2020 2:30 PM
To: Charlotte Smith Andrews, VPAA
CC: W. Ways, Chair of Humanities and Social Sciences
Subject: English and Writing program

Dear Dr. Smith Andrews,

As I previously mentioned to you, eight years ago, at the request of the previous administration, I began the process of redesigning and updating the English and writing program. Over the course of six years, I met with all stakeholders to incorporate their ideas and address their concerns. Two years ago, the new program went before our educational policies committee and was approved in late 2019. At that point, it was sent to the president's office, and we have not heard another word about it. Do you know what happened to our proposal?

Pamela

From: Charlotte Smith Andrews, VPAA
Tues 11/3/2020 2:40 PM
To: Pankhurst, Pamela
CC: W. Ways, Chair of Humanities and Social Sciences
Subject: English and Writing program

Dear Pamela,

After hours of searching I was able to track down the proposal. President Moto-Lenovo decided not to advance this proposal last April.

Remain energized!

Charlotte

From: Pankhurst, Pamela
Tues 11/3/2020 2:45 PM
To: Charlotte Smith Andrews, VPAA
CC: W. Ways, Chair of Humanities and Social Sciences
Subject: English and Writing program

Dear Charlotte,

Elaine killed our proposal and we're just being told about that now? Can you make a case for her to reconsider it?

Pamela

From: Charlotte Smith Andrews, VPAA
Wed 11/4/2020 11:30 PM
To: Pankhurst, Pamela
CC: W. Ways, Chair of Humanities and Social Sciences
Subject: English and Writing program

Dear Pamela,

It was the responsibility of the previous dean to convey this information to you. I'm sorry that his questionable practices have delayed this process. However, I cannot support the proposal. I have reviewed it thoroughly and agree with President Moto-Lenovo that our students will find this program boring and unappealing.

Better luck next time, and remain energized!

Charlotte

From: Pankhurst, Pamela
Wed 11/4/2020 11:45 PM
To: Charlotte Smith Andrews, VPAA
CC: W. Ways, Chair of Humanities and Social Sciences
Subject: English and Writing program

Dear Charlotte,

~~BORING? What kind of {swear word omitted} criticism is that~~

Could you elaborate on your assessment of the work that we spent eight years on and got approved at every level as "boring and unappealing"?

Pamela

From: Charlotte Smith Andrews, VPAA
Thurs 11/5/2020 1:30 AM
To: Pankhurst, Pamela
CC: W. Ways, Chair of Humanities and Social Sciences
Subject: English and Writing program

Dear Pamela,

Your proposal is out of touch with the needs of twenty-first century learners, who aren't interested in taking courses in writing steampunk and space opera, picture books, graphic novels, memoir, screenplays, or writing for the web. They want practical courses in grammar, technical writing, promotional writing, business writing, and writing for newspapers. Do some research on competitive programs in our region, state, and nation and consider modeling your proposal after one of those. Create a program that everyone can support! Writing is my discipline and I have seen, and even designed, much more dynamic programs that remain highly successful! I know you can do it too!

Remain energized!

Charlotte

From: Pankhurst, Pamela
Thurs 11/5/2020 1:35 AM
To: Patel, Raj
Subject: FWD: English and Writing program

Sorry to send this IN THE MIDDLE OF THE NIGHT but Charlotte just sent it to me. Look at this list of courses she thinks we should offer! Writing for newspapers? It's like she's accessing a totally outdated database! And anyway, students won't take any of these courses—we quit offering them because nobody enrolls. They just sign up to be on the staff of Buck's online newspaper where no one holds them accountable for making sure that their reporting is accurate.

From: Raj Patel, Chair of the Division of BESOD
Thurs 11/5/2020 10:00 AM
To: Pankhurst, Pamela
Subject: FWD: English and Writing program

Oh brother! I can't even!

From: Pankhurst, Pamela
Thurs 11/5/2020 10:01 AM
To: Charlotte Smith Andrews VPAA
CC: W. Ways, Chair of Humanities and Social Sciences
Subject: Writing Program

Dear Dr. Smith Andrews,

I am writing to clarify your comments about the writing program revision that was turned down by President Moto-Lenovo. I'd like to design a new program that everyone can support, but I'm hoping for more input from you. Could you clarify what you'd like to see in a revised program?

You mention that writing is your field and that you've revised programs elsewhere that are now successful. Could you point me to some of those programs? I was unaware that you have credentials in creative writing and I'm very interested in looking at some of your publications—do you have any links to them? I welcome all of the ways that your background can help us to improve our programs.

We do need to move quickly, since our program hasn't been updated in fourteen years and our enrollment is likely to continue declining.

Best,

Pamela

From: Charlotte Smith Andrews, VPAA
Thurs 11/5/2020 10:00 PM
To: Pankhurst, Pamela
CC: W. Ways, Chair of Humanities and Social Sciences
Subject: Writing Program

Hi Pamela,

The question isn't what I want. It's what YOU want. I believe that all writing is creative, but you can access some of my work in the *Chronicle of the Highly Educated*. Please see the links below.

Remain energized!

Charlotte

Links:

<u>Who's the Boss? Revisioning Academic Structures to Enhance Administrative Power</u>

<u>Votes of No Confidence: There's Got to Be a Better Way</u>

<u>Restraining orders against the Administration: The Outsized Defensiveness of Faculty Scholars</u>

From: Pankhurst, Pamela
Fri 11/6/2020 10:00 AM
To: Raj Patel, Chair of the Division of BESOD
Subject: FWD: Writing Program

OMG take a look at these links.

From: Raj Patel, Chair of the Division of BESOD
Fri 11/6/2020 10:30 AM
To: Pankhurst, Pamela
Subject: FWD: Writing Program

OMG

Moving Up in Academia: What to Pack for Your Next Power Trip

From: Pankhurst, Pamela
Fri 11/6/2020 2:30 PM
To: Charlotte Smith Andrews, VPAA
CC: W. Ways, Chair of Humanities and Social Sciences
Subject: Writing Program

Dear Charlotte,

Thank you for these links. I agree that all writing is creative, as are many other endeavors, but we're trying to design a program related to the specific field that is called Creative Writing. And quite frankly, I need your input because I'm reluctant to spend another eight years on paperwork that you're going to turn down. It seems to me that since you've been involved in revising writing programs elsewhere, our program proposal could benefit from this experience. Thank you for any suggestions.

Best,

Pamela

From: Charlotte Smith Andrews, VPAA
Fri 11/7/2020 12:45 AM
To: Pankhurst, Pamela
CC: W. Ways, Chair of Humanities and Social Sciences
Subject: Writing Program

Hi Pamela,

As the program director for writing, this is your job. It is not up to me to do your job. However, if you make an appointment with Kinsey, we can discuss your ideas.

Remain energized!

Charlotte

From: Millhouse, Kinsey
Wed 11/11/2020 9:00 AM
To: Pankhurst, Pamela
Subject: FWD: Writing Program

Vice President Andrews will need to cancel the meeting we scheduled yesterday for tomorrow to discuss the writing program. We will reschedule as soon as possible.

From: Craig, Brittney
Mon 11/16/2020 9:00 AM
To: Pankhurst, Pamela
Subject: Advising

I'm really confused. I just got this message from the dean:

> Dr. Pankhurst told you to take the Writing Capstone next semester, but in fact I've looked at your transcript and you do not need Writing Capstone. Even though you are a writing major, I see that you enrolled in Engineering Capstone when you were a

freshman. There is no need to complete two Capstones. Please disregard the advice you were given.

But I'm an English and writing major and I didn't actually finish the Engineering Capstone and I have to complete Writing Capstone to graduate so what should I do?

Brittney

From: Pankhurst, Pamela
Mon 11/16/2020 9:05 AM
To: Raj Patel, Chair of the Division of BESOD
Subject: FWD: Advising

ARGH

From: Pankhurst, Pamela
Mon 11/16/2020 9:30 AM
To: Craig, Brittney
Subject: Advising

Brittney,

Just enroll in the class. The system is not going to let you graduate until you complete it.

Prof. Pankhurst
From: Craig, Brittney
Mon 11/16/2020 10:00 AM
To: Pankhurst, Pamela
Subject: Advising

But am I going to get in trouble with the dean?

From: Pankhurst, Pamela
Mon 11/16/2020 11:00 AM
To: Craig, Brittney
Subject: Advising

She was just telling you that in her estimation, you don't need it, but according to the system, you do. So I would guess that whether or not you "need" it, you will WANT to take it in order to graduate. The administration won't forbid anyone from taking a class they WANT to take. So just enroll.

Prof. Pankhurst

From: Pankhurst, Pamela
Mon 11/16/2020 11:05 AM
To: Raj Patel, Chair of the Division of BESOD
Subject: FWD: Advising

Now I feel sneaky and underhanded telling a student to take the class that's a requirement for her program. Also, did you see? Charlotte just called a meeting for the day before Thanksgiving.

...

December 2020
Professor Pamela Pankhurst To-Do List

- Mark finals
- ~~Turn in final grades~~
- Fill out incomplete forms

- ~~Meet with Dean about program revisions~~
- Put spring courses on Whiplash
- Buy children's potholder loom and yarn loops
- Make 15 potholders in different colors and patterns (stress relief)
- Send Clarissa a Christmas card
- Work on creative work/song lyrics
- Clean out Roomba
- COLLAPSE AND SLEEP FOR A WEEK

Grease, Sr.
Alternate Title: *Rogaine*
Maturely, Securely Devoted to You, performed by Sandy
(To the Tune of "Hopelessly Devoted to You")

Guess mine's not the first pacemaker? Drop in

Estrogen?

My eyes not the first to be gritty and dry...

UGH I'm hopelessly stuck on this one...

From: The Office of President Elaine J. Moto-Lenovo
Wed 12/08/2020 2:00 PM
To: Faculty and Staff
CC: Charlotte Smith Andrews, VPAA
Subject: Grave concerns

Dear Faculty and Staff,

It has come to my attention that our placement rate is the lowest one among westernnorth Pennsylvania small liberal arts colleges. The facts that we are in a rural, isolated, and impoverished area, that our students last year graduated in the midst of a pandemic and therefore had no mobility whatsoever, that we only just now hired a director of placement after a year-long vacancy, and that we are the only small liberal arts college in Northwestern Pennsylvania are not adequate excuses for this poor rate of post graduate placement.

It is incumbent on you to bring your energy and resources to changing these alarming statistics, even if it means postponing your holiday celebrations and foregoing relaxation.

Have a rejuvenating holiday season!

Elaine

From: Raj Patel, Chair of the Division of BESOD
Wed 12/08/2020 2:30 PM
To: Pankhurst, Pamela
Subject: FWD: Grave concerns

Westernnorth PA?

From: Charlotte Smith Andrews, VPAA
Thurs 12/09/2020 2:00 PM
To: Faculty and Staff
Subject: Congratulations!

Dear Faculty and Staff,

I'm pleased to inform you that Dr. Holden Carfield, hired as our new placement director last month, will be leaving us for other exciting opportunities in the academic enterprise.

Remain energized!

Charlotte

From: Millhouse, Kinsey
Wed 12/16/2020 9:00 AM
To: Pankhurst, Pamela
CC: Charlotte Smith Andrews, VPAA
Subject: FWD: Writing Program

Vice President Andrews will need to cancel the meeting for tomorrow to discuss the writing program. We will reschedule as soon as possible.

From: Pankhurst, Pamela
Wed 12/16/2020 9:30 AM
To: Raj Patel, Chair of the Division of BESOD; Patel, Saanvi
Subject: OMG

OMG, I'm coming over. Not only have they chased Holden away, but the dean just cancelled a THIRD meeting with me. I can't even.

...

January 2021
Professor Pamela Pankhurst To-Do List

- Finish putting spring classes on Whiplash

- ~~Mark incomplete work~~
- Meet with dean about program revisions
- Opening week meetings
- Phone call with Clarissa!
- Order more potholder loops
- Practice jiujitsu
- Work on creative work/song lyrics

From: Charlotte Smith Andrews, VPAA
Mon 1/04/2021 1:00 AM
To: SLAC Faculty
Subject: Opening Week

Dear Faculty,

I trust that you had a relaxing break with self-health as your priority! We kept meetings to a minimum, as you may have noted, only requiring you to be at one pandemic preparedness meeting on Christmas Eve and one diversity strategy meeting on New Year's Day.

Now we are all excited to gear up for the new semester! We will be holding mandatory meetings from 9:00-5:00 Monday-Saturday January 11-16 to prepare for the new term, with meaningful engagement planned in a variety of information vistas to enhance the educational experience and center strategic informational flows and feedback loops. We will discuss how these piggyback and dovetail with each other as well as foundational protocols, and how we can enhance our deliverables over the course of the next semester.

All faculty should prepare a 20-minute PowerPoint presentation highlighting your innovative teaching techniques from the fall. Please submit these to me no later than tomorrow, January 5, at 5 p.m.

Remain energized!

Charlotte

From: Millhouse, Kinsey
Wed 1/06/2021 9:30 AM
To: Pankhurst, Pamela
CC: Charlotte Smith Andrews, VPAA
Subject: Meeting Request

Vice President Andrews will need to cancel the meeting for tomorrow to discuss the writing program. We will reschedule as soon as possible.

From: W. Ways, Chair of Humanities and Social Sciences
Wed 1/06/2020 7:00 AM
To: Pankhurst, Pamela
Subject: Shutdown of the English and writing program

Pamela,

Please don't shoot the messenger here, but I just got out of a meeting with the dean. She told me that she is putting English and writing in hibernation because our programs are embarrassingly outdated. There simply aren't enough students right now to sustain a major, and she said that we will be putting a hold on the program until we manage to revise the program, build our numbers, and bring in more students. I asked her how we were supposed to build our numbers if we can't advertise or accept new students, and she said, "It's your job to figure that out."

I'm sorry not to have better news.

Wily

From: Pankhurst, Pamela
Wed 1/06/2021 7:30 AM
To: Charlotte Smith Andrews, VPAA
CC: W. Ways, Chair of Humanities and Social Sciences
Subject: English and Writing program

Dear Dr. Smith Andrews,

I received a bewildering communication from my chair, Dr. Ways, saying that you were shutting down the English and writing program. Can you please clarify what this means? During our process of interviewing administrative candidates, we have always emphasized the importance of collaboration and transparency, yet I keep receiving vital and incomplete information about my program secondhand.

I have made four appointments with you to discuss the program, all of which have been canceled at the last minute. I would appreciate more information about your plans for the writing major. Attached please find a list of possible alternatives for revising and updating our program, based on a comprehensive assessment of other programs in the area, as a starting place for a conversation. See single-spaced 30-page attachment.

Pamela

From: Charlotte Smith Andrews, VPAA
Thurs 1/07/2021 2:00 AM
To: Pankhurst, Pamela
CC: W. Ways, Chair of Humanities and Social Sciences
Subject: English and Writing program

Hi Pamela

Today, I am starting from the top of the email inbox, so your message just appeared. I hope that your week has been both productive and pleasant.

First, I am not sure what you mean by this first paragraph, especially the highlighted portion [highlights, mine]:

During our process of interviewing administrator candidates, we have always emphasized the importance of collaboration and transparency, yet I keep receiving vital and incomplete information about my program secondhand.

Let me be clear—your first line of communication and information is with the Division Chair, Dr. Ways, so I do not know what you are referring to as 'secondhand' information. I am happy to meet after you have initial discussions about division matters with the chair first; we can then meet collectively.

I have copied Wily so we can have the collaboration and transparency that you so correctly lift in your email.

Remain energized,

Charlotte

From: Pankhurst, Pamela
Thurs 1/07/2021 2:30 AM
To: Charlotte Smith Andrews, VPAA
CC: W. Ways, Chair of Humanities and Social Sciences
Subject: English and Writing program

Dear Charlotte,

I hope that your week has been super superbly delightful. Wily was in fact my first line of communication, but he was unable to give me any further information. I await your valuable input and more information about where to go from here.

Pamela

From: Pankhurst, Pamela
Wed 1/13/2021 1:00 PM
To: W. Ways, Chair of Humanities and Social Sciences
Subject: Shutdown of the English and writing program

Hi Wily,

As you can see, I'm writing this message during the training on diversity with a focus on avoiding reverse racism. Since you have your camera off, I assume you also are doing business rather than paying attention. (Since we're not allowed to call on our students, I assume that the administration isn't allowed to call on us either, right?)

I'm still waiting for an answer from Charlotte to my questions from last week, but all I've gotten was her completely opaque response to my concerns about transparency. I don't have any idea how I'm supposed to plan for the fall or what my job is if my program doesn't exist.

Pamela

From: Pankhurst, Pamela
Wed 1/13/2021 1:15 PM
To: Raj Patel, Chair of the Division of BESOD
Subject: I give up

Are you in this meeting? I don't see you. So, anyway, I think I'm going to take early retirement and go live on a deserted island somewhere and lounge under palm trees eating Cheetos. I mean, it's absurd to expect one person to recruit for and maintain a program, designing and teaching all of its courses and advising all related student organizations when the program has little visibility or administrative support. It's a losing battle.

Oh, screw it. I'm turning off my camera, my mic, and my sound, minimizing the Zoom screen so that our dean is just a tiny square in the corner of my computer, and working on my creative work. That way, I can sing the lyrics as I write them, except during the parts where our colleagues do presentations on their teaching. I forgot to submit mine, whoops, did you?

Grease, Sr.
Alternate Title: *Rogaine*
Routine Procedure
(To the Tune of "Summer Lovin," cont'd)

(Danny:)

She walked by me, she had a cane

(Sandy:)

He sat beside me, began to mansplain

(Danny:)

I saved her life, she almost fell

(Sandy:)

He grabbed my arm, I said what the hell

(Together:)

Twilight sleep made him (me) seem less a creep

Cause oh, oh, that anesthesia

(Danny:)

We went to bingo, had lots of fun

(Sandy:)

Then got lost due to poor night vision

(Danny:)

We made out, our hearing aids popped

(Sandy:)

We stayed out till five o'clock

(Together:)

Twilight sleep high, tricking our eyes

Cause oh oh that anesthesia

(Male chorus:)

Tell me more, tell me more

Did she give you a thrill

(Female chorus:)

Tell me more, tell me more

Are you in his will?

From: Raj Patel, Chair of the Division of BESOD
Wed 1/13/2021 5:15 PM
To: Pankhurst, Pamela
Subject: I give up

Oh, sorry, I turned off my camera and mic and hummed Hindustani and Carnatic music while doing yoga all afternoon. Caught a few seconds of Walter Kotzwinkle's session on "High Credit, Low Commitment Resume Padding," Alma's "Improving Classroom Concentration and Agility through Backward Walking Breaks," and Jon Sagal's "Riding the Winds to Higher Planes of Existence via Zoom Background Design." Did you notice that Charlotte left the meeting as soon as the faculty presentations began?

From: The Office of President Elaine J. Moto-Lenovo
Thurs 1/14/2021 2:00 PM
To: Faculty and Staff
Subject: Moderation of E-mail Lists

Dear Faculty and Staff,

From here on out, VPAA Charlotte Smith Andrews will moderate all e-mail that is sent to the Faculty and Staff lists. We take this step to ensure that no one's inboxes are loadedover with messages and you can focus on the most essential communications from our campus. We have also removed all adjuncts and emeritus professors from the list to relieve them of the burden of campus communications.

Thank you, VPAA Andrews for assuming this very important role.

Elaine

From: Pankhurst, Pamela
Thurs 1/14/2021 2:30 PM
To: Raj Patel, Chair of the Division of BESOD
Subject: Is This Weird?

She did it again! Loadedover instead of over-loaded? She's always doing that. Westernnorth when she means northwestern? Desist and cease instead of cease and desist? 19 Covid? Track Fast? Is this a form of dyslexia or what? Or just an attempt to distract us from the fact that they are now **censoring our e-mail!** (Oh, and did you hear—they cancelled the student newspaper, since they don't believe in freedom of speech. Should we be protesting or applauding this move?)

From: W. Ways, Chair of Humanities and Social Sciences
Mon 1/18/2021 6:00 AM
To: Pankhurst, Pamela
Subject: Shutdown of the English and writing program

Hi Pamela,

Welcome to the new semester! Dr. Andrews says that she will meet with our unit to discuss our programs after we all compile 30-page single spaced reports on competitive programs in our area.

Wily

From: Pankhurst, Pamela
Wed 1/18/2021 9:00 AM
To: W. Ways, Chair of Humanities and Social Sciences
Subject: Shutdown of the English and writing program

I already did that, attached to my e-mail of 1/6. She didn't read it.

I'll just copy it and send it again.

From: Charlotte Smith Andrews, VPAA
Thurs 1/18/2021
To: Pankhurst, Pamela
CC: W. Ways, Chair of Humanities and Social Sciences
Subject: English and Writing program

[crickets]

From: Charlotte Smith Andrews, VPAA
Sun 1/21/2021 11:59 PM
To: Faculty
Subject: Black History Month

Dear Colleagues,

February is Black History Month, and we must all be cognizant of the importance of retaining the tuition dollars of our students of color. Toward that end, I invite faculty to submit 20-minute Zoom lunchtime PowerPoint presentations on some aspect of black history. Even if your research has nothing to do with race issues, please insert some reference to them.

Remain energized!

With boundless compassion for all of humanity,

Charlotte

...

February 2021
Professor Pamela Pankhurst To-Do List

- Read
- Prepare
- Teach
- Grade
- Read
- Prepare
- Teach
- Grade
- Paperwork
- Conferences
- Meeting with dean?
- Try to convince students to turn on cameras on Zoom
- Go to lunchtime Black History Month presentations
- Zoom jiujitsu blue belt award ceremony
- Zoom date with Clarissa!

Grease, Sr.
Alternate Title: *Rogaine*
"Stranded at the Social Security Office,"
performed by Danny
(To the Tune of "Stranded at the Drive-in")

~~Stranded at the social security office, without a~~

~~comb-~~

~~over~~

Stranded at the social security office, branded a

chrome dome

What will they say at the assisted living home

ARGH

From: Charlotte Smith Andrews, VPAA
Mon 2/1/2021 3:00 AM
To: Faculty and Staff
Subject: Black History Month

Dear Colleagues,

We have a robust lineup of presentations to celebrate Black History Month. Dr. Alma Revers Arden will present on "Little-known African American Contributions to the Backward Walking Movement," Dr. Ways will present on "Abolishing Failing Grades: How Promoting the Dunning-Kruger Effect in Overrepresented Populations Trickles Down to Benefit Everybody," and Dr. Baker will discuss "Diverse Classrooms: The Epistemology of Architectonic Structurates." And last but not least, Dr. Usman Amadi will give a talk titled "The Turing Test and the Abolishment of Racial Differences through Technology." They will be held over lunch on Zoom this Thursday, 2/4, from 11:30-1:00. I hope to see you all there!

Remain energized!

Charlotte

From: Charlotte Smith Andrews, VPAA
Tues 2/2/2021 1:30 AM
To: Faculty Mentoring Circle
Subject: Meeting

Dear Inaugural Members of our Faculty Mentoring Circle,

Our first meeting will be held on Zoom this Thursday, 2/4, from 11:30-1:00. I will be organizing breakout rooms so that you can chat with your mentees— no need to worry about scheduling these meetings yourself at your own convenience!

Remain energized!

Charlotte

From: Charlotte Smith Andrews, VPAA
Tues 2/2/2021 7:00 PM
To: Faculty Development Committee
Subject: Meeting

Dear Faculty Development Committee,

You will be meeting from 11:45-1:00 on Thursday 2/4 to start evaluating spring grant applications. You will be receiving a Zoom link soon.

Remain energized!

Charlotte

From: Charlotte Smith Andrews, VPAA
Wed 2/3/2021 12:01 AM
To: Staff
Subject: Parking issues

Dear Staff,

While finding parking places has not been a huge issue during the pandemic, we know that it will be again when in-person class delivery resumes. Therefore, we will be holding a forum for you to air your parking grievances tomorrow from 11:30-12:45. Please reserve that time slot for this very important activity.

Remain energized!

Charlotte

From: Charlotte Smith Andrews, VPAA
Thurs 2/4/2021 5:00 PM
To: Faculty and Staff
Subject: Black History Month

It has come to my attention that attendance at our inaugural Black History Month faculty presentations was abysmal. I am ashamed of our campus's lack of support for this important initiative. Please be informed that in the future your participation in such events is mandatory.

Remain energized!

Charlotte

From: W. Ways, Chair of Humanities and Social Sciences
Mon 2/8/2021 8:00 AM
To: Pankhurst, Pamela
Subject: E-mail concerns

Hi Pamela,

I'm going to text you my g-mail address. Please address all future correspondence to that address.

Wily

From: pp@gmail.com
Mon 2/8/2021 9:00 AM
To: ww@gmail.com
Subject: E-mail concerns

Hi Wily,

So you actually think that the administration is monitoring our e-mail? Why would they read our e-mail? They don't even read their own.

Pamela

From: Pankhurst, Pamela
Mon 2/8/2021 9:30 AM
To: Raj Patel, Chair of the Division of BESOD
Subject: E-mail concerns

Hey, did you hear that everyone's communicating through g-mail now because they're afraid the administration is spying on us? (HEY ADMINISTRATORS, if you're reading this, good! I've got some things I want you to hear, so please, read away! Everyone feels that you are taking advantage of our pandemic isolation to make hostile decisions. We are all frustrated, depressed, and demoralized. The atmosphere on campus is toxic. If you're reading this, PLEASE DO SOMETHING!)

From: bb@gmail.com
Wed 2/10/2021 6:00 PM
To: tenuredfaculty@gmail.com
Subject: E-mail concerns

Tenured faculty across content and curricular areas who share cognitive and experiential disequilibrium wish to orchestrate a gathering for us to actualize our concerns. Please distribute this informational messaging to the appropriate constituencies.

Buck

From: wk@gmail.com
Wed 2/10/2021 6:15 PM
To: tenuredfaculty@gmail.com
Subject: E-mail concerns

So you're saying we should all meet to figure out what to do? Nobody from my area is willing to meet on Zoom. They're afraid of being recorded. We'd like to meet in a park at 8 a.m. Saturday morning.

Walter

From: pp@gmail.com
Wed 2/10/2021 6:30 PM
To: tenuredfaculty@gmail.com
Subject: E-mail concerns

Morale is at an all-time low, everyone is worried about their jobs, and our students are terrified that they won't be allowed to graduate. I agree that we've got to do something but it's supposed to be 3 degrees at 8 a.m. on Saturday morning. Can't we just meet on Zoom? It announces when it's recording.

Pamela

From: wk@gmail.com
Thurs 2/11/2021 6:45 PM
To: tenuredfaculty@gmail.com
Subject: E-mail concerns

But what if someone records on their phone?

Walter

From: pp@gmail.com
Thurs 2/11/2021 6:50 PM
To: tenuredfaculty@gmail.com
Subject: E-mail concerns

So what if they do? And couldn't they record a meeting in the park? Wouldn't it be a win for us if the administration cares enough to eavesdrop on our conversation? It's not like we're going to say anything behind their backs that we wouldn't say to their faces.

Pamela

From: jls@gmail.com
Thurs 2/11/2021 7:00 PM
To: tenuredfaculty@gmail.com
Subject: E-mail concerns

We have to be very careful. Tenured people everywhere are losing their jobs. I have two kids to put through college, and my husband lost his job because of the pandemic.

Jonathan

From: Pankhurst, Pamela
Fri 2/12/2021 1:00 PM
To: Charlotte Smith Andrews, VPAA
CC: Office of the President Elaine J. Moto-Lenovo
Subject: Invitation to Student Magazine Release

Dear Dean Smith Andrews and President Moto-Lenovo,

On Wednesday, February 17 at 7:00 p.m., we will unveil our new issue of our award-winning literary magazine during a Zoom celebration and open mic. It would mean a great deal to the students to have you both attend and perhaps even say a few words. I recognize that your schedules are extremely busy but want to assure you that students would be gratified even by the briefest of appearances if you can't stay for the whole event.

Pamela

From: Charlotte Smith Andrews, VPAA
Mon 2/15/2021
To: Pankhurst, Pamela
Subject: Invitation to Student Magazine Release

[deafening silence]

From: Office of the President Elaine J. Moto-Lenovo
Mon 2/15/2021
To: Pankhurst, Pamela
Subject: Invitation to Student Magazine Release

[crickets]

From: Pankhurst, Pamela
Mon 2/15/2021 11:00 AM
To: Raj Patel, Chair of the Division of BESOD
Subject: Invitation to Student Magazine Release

Here is Charlotte and Elaine's response to my open mic invitation:

From: Raj Patel, Chair of the Division of BESOD
Thurs 2/18/2021 8:00 AM
To: Pankhurst, Pamela
Subject: Invitation to Student Magazine Release

I wanted to come to your open mic last night and hum some songs, but Charlotte called a mandatory chairs meeting at that time.

From: Pankhurst, Pamela
Thurs 2/18/2021 9:00 AM
To: Raj Patel, Chair of the Division of BESOD
Subject: Invitation to Student Magazine Release

It's OK, we had a great turnout. A hundred people, with thirty performing. Lots of music, comedy acts, poetry, dramatic re-enactments of scenes from original fantasy fiction, students who shared their screens to show us graphic novels and comics. It was amazing! They asked if we'd organize another one.

From: Office of Student Engagement
Sun 2/21/2021 2:30 AM
To: Faculty and Staff
Subject: Zoom dance party!

We'll be holding a Zoom dance party fundraiser on Saturday, 2/20/21 at 7:30 PM. Please everyone Zoom in, show your support for our students, and make this a success!

From: Campus Bookstore
Sun 2/21/2021 2:30 AM
To: Faculty and Staff
Subject: Friday only sale!

The bookstore will be giving 50 percent off on all campus sweatshirts Friday 2/19/21 ONLY. Come buy yours!

From: Campus Nurse
Sun 2/21/2021 2:30 AM
To: Faculty and Staff
Subject: Campus Super Spreader Event

On Wednesday, 2/17/21, 300 students received positive COVID tests, 30 have been hospitalized, and four died. If you appeared in person on campus any time in the last two weeks we strongly advise that you be tested repeatedly over the next ten days while remaining in isolation.

From: Raj Patel, Chair of the Division of BESOD
Sun 2/21/2021 10:00 AM
To: Pankhurst, Pamela
Subject: Time warp?

Did you get a series of announcements early this morning for events that are already over?

From: Pankhurst, Pamela
Sun 2/21/2021 10:15 AM
To: Raj Patel, Chair of the Division of BESOD
Subject: FWD: Time warp?

Charlotte forgot to moderate them until today!

From: Charlotte Smith Andrews, VPAA
Mon 2/22/2021 2:30 AM
To: Faculty, Staff, and Students
Subject: Black History Month

Dear Students, Staff, and Faculty,

Noble Prize-winning poet and my personal friend Dodd McKown, whose first wife was mixed-race, has agreed to speak to us via Zoom in a special event for Black History Month. We are so fortunate that despite his busy schedule, he was able to grant us a one-hour slot for only $20,000.

His talk will be held on Wednesday, February 24 from 5:00-6:00 PM. Faculty, please excuse students from class for this very important event. Staff should expect to remain at work an extra two hours to support this event, and I expect a robust faculty turnout!

Remain energized!

Charlotte

From: Raj Patel, Chair of the Division of BESOD
Wed 2/24/2021 5:08 PM
To: Pankhurst, Pamela
Subject: Dodd McKown

Are you at this Zoom event? Oh, my god. The sound isn't working. I'm cringing.

From: Maus, Ralph S.
Wed 2/24/2021 5:12 PM
To: Division of Humanities and Social Sciences
Subject: Dodd McKown

Are you all watching this? They can't get the sound to work! Can you believe that nobody did a technical run through before this event?

From: Abubakar, Obi
Fri 2/24/2020 PM
To: Division of Humanities and Social Sciences
Subject: How Embarrassing

From: Zuckerman, Wilbur
Wed 2/24/2021 5:15 PM
To: Division of Humanities and Social Sciences
Subject: Dodd McKown

Has anyone actually ever heard of this guy? I haven't heard of him and I can't hear him either.

From: Sagal, Jonathan L.
Wed 2/24/2021 5:20 PM
To: Division of Humanities and Social Sciences
Subject: Dowd McKown

Is this guy actually calling in on his phone to mumble poetry to us while staring at us on Zoom? This is a total shitshow!

From: Kotzwinkle, Walter
Wed 2/24/2021 5:30 PM
To: Pankhurst, Pamela
Subject: This Poet Guy

I tuned in late and I keep turning up my sound but I can't hear anything. There's this guy muttering at us. Is there something wrong with my equipment? When you're chair, can you tell Mrs. Andrews that we're not going to attend these embarrassing events?

From: W. Ways, Chair of Humanities and Social Sciences
Wed 2/24/2021 5:35 PM
To: Division of Humanities and Social Sciences
Subject: Disaster!

From: Kim, Jeo-Yun
Wed 2/24/2021 5:40 PM
To: Pankhurst, Pamela
Subject: I'm cringing!

From: Baker, Buck
Wed 2/24/2021 5:45 PM
To: Pankhurst, Pamela
Subject: What the Hell????

From: Charlotte Smith Andrews, VPAA
Wed 2/25/2021 2:30 AM
To: Faculty, Staff, and Students
Subject: Technical Difficulties :(

Dear Students, Staff, and Faculty,

What a great turnout we had for that marvelous presentation by social justice warrior Dodd McKown! I know you were all inspired. We're going to bring him back again for Women's History Month for those of you who couldn't get your sound to work.

What does he have to tell us about the female experience? Well, plenty—he's had four wives! Please reserve next Wednesday, 3/3/21 at 5:00 PM for this very special encore presentation. Faculty, please once again excuse students from class for this very important event. Staff should expect to remain at work an extra two hours to support this event, and I expect another robust faculty turnout!

Remain energized!

Charlotte

...

March 2021
Professor Pamela Pankhurst To-Do List

- Find time to make To-Do list

From: Charlotte Smith Andrews, VPAA
Wed 3/3/2021 10:00 PM
To: Faculty, Staff, and Students
Subject: Dodd McKown

Dear Students, Staff, and Faculty,

It's 5:00 PM and the Dodd McKown encore event is starting right now! Please log on!

Charlotte

From: Raj Patel, Chair of the Division of BESOD
Wed 3/3/2021 10:15 PM
To: Pankhurst, Pamela
Subject: Time warp!

OMG she forgot to moderate her own message until four hours after the event was over!

From: W. Ways, Chair of Humanities and Social Sciences
Thurs 3/4/2021 8:00 AM
To: Program Directors, Division of Humanities and Social Sciences
Subject: Fall Schedule

Dean Andrews has asked us to submit fall schedules for our programs by 8:00 AM tomorrow. I will have Sally put last year's schedules in your mailboxes so you can use those as starting points.

From: Pankhurst, Pamela
Thurs 3/4/2021 9:00 AM
To: W. Ways, Chair of Humanities and Social Sciences
Subject: Fall Schedule

Hi Wily,

We have been asked to submit our fall schedules, but I have many questions.

1. There's a rumor that the president is going to dissolve all divisions, so what if I'm not chair after all? We need to schedule three classes at times I can teach them but also at times when adjuncts can pick them up.
2. However, there's a rumor that the president is going to abolish some or all adjunct positions. In the event of the loss of adjuncts, Arthur's class needs to be at a time when

Dora can teach it, and Dora's class needs to be at a time that Arthur can teach it.
3. But Arthur's classes need to be all on TTh, since he's scheduled for comp on those days and has an hour commute, and Dora's classes need to be all on MWF, since she's scheduled for comp on those days and has a two-hour commute.
4. If neither of them will be employed by the university, and I'm chair, we need someone else to teach the classes.
5. If instead I'm not chair but the classes are cancelled for lack of enrollment, I will need something to teach.
6. And finally, if there is no program, no classes, and no one to teach them, what's the name of the bus driver?

From: Charlotte Smith Andrews, VPAA
Wed 3/4/2021 11:45 AM
To: Preparing Global Citizens Committee
Subject: Next Meeting

Dear Committee,

We will meet on Friday at 4:30 PM via Zoom to begin our discussion of strategies for preparing all of our students to be globally engaged citizens. We all agree that in this interconnected and interdependent world, students need the awareness, skills, and knowledge to understand, navigate, and flourish.

Please prepare your SWOT analysis to present on Friday, and please be sure that each item is in the appropriate column. Note: we will not be discussing the cancellation of all foreign languages, including the Spanish, French, Chinese, and Russian language programs. These are personnel matters that are not relevant to our discussion.)

Remain energized!

With boundless compassion for all of humanity,

Charlotte

From: Pankhurst, Pamela
Wed 3/4/2021 1:00 PM
To: Raj Patel, Chair of the Division of BESOD
Subject: Preparing Global Citizens Committee

Wait, what does SWOT stand for? Strengths, weaknesses, opportunities and—tactics? Targets? Threats?

From: Raj Patel, Chair of the Division of BESOD
Wed 3/4/2021 1:15 PM
To: Pankhurst, Pamela
Subject: Preparing Global Citizens Committee

Strategic Waste Of Time

From: Pankhurst, Pamela
Fri 3/05/2021 4:35 PM
To: Charlotte Smith Andrews, VPAA
CC: W. Ways, Chair of Humanities and Social Sciences
Subject: Concerns about Fall Scheduling

Dear Charlotte,

Professor Ways tells me that during a meeting with you earlier today, you changed the terms of the agreement we had made before I agreed to run for chair of our division and put three courses on the fall schedule for me. When we met in November, you agreed that I would keep my research course release and would only teach one class as chair. I am concerned that I will be unable to fulfill the role of chair without the time to continue my creative work.

Pamela

From: Charlotte Smith Andrews, VPAA
Fri 3/5/2021 4:58 PM
To: Pankhurst, Pamela
CC: W. Ways, Chair of Humanities and Social Sciences
Subject: Concerns about Fall Scheduling

Hi Pamela,

If you have a letter from the Dean of Academic Affairs about a long-term leave arrangement, it comes from predecessors.

I can meet with you along with your chair this evening after the current meeting I am in at present.

If you can meet today, I will send a meeting invite as soon as this meeting ends.

Remain energized!

Dr. Charlotte Smith Andrews
VPAA

From: Pankhurst, Pamela
Fri 3/05/2021 5:00 PM
To: Charlotte Smith Andrews, VPAA
CC: W. Ways, Chair of Humanities and Social Sciences
Subject: Concerns about Fall Scheduling
Hi Charlotte,

Yes, of course my agreement comes from predecessors. It's a course release agreement, not a long-term leave agreement. I am available to meet anytime.

Pamela

From: Charlotte Smith Andrews, VPAA
Fri 3/05/2021 6:10 PM
To: Pankhurst, Pamela
CC: W. Ways, Chair of Humanities and Social Sciences
Subject: Concerns about Fall Scheduling

Please join a Zoom meeting at this link.

From: Pankhurst, Pamela
Fri 3/05/2021 6:16 PM
To: Charlotte Smith Andrews, VPAA
Subject: Concerns about Fall Scheduling

Trying to access this meeting but don't see a passcode

From: Pankhurst, Pamela
Fri 3/05/2021 6:18 PM
To: Charlotte Smith Andrews, VPAA
CC: W. Ways, Chair of Humanities and Social Sciences, Millhouse, Kinsey
Subject: Concerns about Fall Scheduling

Hi,

I received a meeting invite but can't get in because I can't find a passcode. Does anybody have one?

Pamela

From: Charlotte Smith Andrews, VPAA
Fri 3/05/2021 6:20 PM
To: Pankhurst, Pamela
CC: W. Ways, Chair of Humanities and Social Sciences, Millhouse, Kinsey
Subject: Concerns about Fall Scheduling

Hi Pamela,

I sent a meeting invitation to address your question, but you must not have considered the matter urgent since you failed to join the meeting. I will have Kinsey schedule us for a meeting on Monday. Your current chair, Wily, will be in the meeting as well.

Enjoy a great weekend and remain energized!

Charlotte

From: Pankhurst, Pamela
Fri 3/05/2021 6:22 PM
To: Charlotte Smith Andrews, VPAA
CC: W. Ways, Chair of Humanities and Social Sciences, Millhouse, Kinsey
Subject: Concerns about Fall Scheduling

Charlotte,

I sent two emails. There was no passcode for the meeting listed, and I couldn't get in.

Pamela

From: Pankhurst, Pamela
Mon 3/08/2021 6:00 PM
To: W. Ways, Chair of Humanities and Social Sciences
Subject: Documentation

Dear Wily,

I am writing this e-mail as a way to document that I have followed the chain of command and committed to writing my concerns and interactions with administration. Please let me know if my summary does not correspond to the way you recall any of these events.

We were abruptly summoned to a meeting this afternoon at 4:00 PM. I explained once again to Dr. Smith Andrews the circumstances of my course reduction. Dr. Smith Andrews stated that the agreement had been made by a previous administration and that she was not legally required to honor it. She denied that our conversation in November had ever occurred. I said that I would be consulting attorneys about the validity of my agreement, but that in the meantime, if the agreement wasn't honored, I would not agree to serve as chair, nor would I have time to perform any service for the university. She told me that I was "belligerent," then directly violated my agreement by putting four courses on the schedule for me for fall.

She then complained that the writing program is stagnant.

"Since you shut it down, how could it be any more dynamic?" I asked.

"I didn't do that," she said. "How would I do that? I don't have the authority to shut down a program."

You then pointed out that she had told you that English and writing were going into hibernation and would not be allowed to accept any new majors.

"That never happened," she said.

I said, "But Wily and I have both written you e-mails referring to the mothballing and shutdown of the program, and you never responded or corrected us."

"I don't respond to inaccurate e-mails," she said.

As we went on to discuss my fall classes, she told me that the way I was teaching my classes was "wrong." She said, "This is my field and you aren't doing it right. You may have thought that what you were doing was working for the last twenty years, but that's not the way we're going to do things." She did not specify what she thought I should be doing differently, but added that my management of the program has been clearly incompetent since we have not enrolled any new students in the last month.

I mentioned the four canceled meetings to discuss the major. She said that she'd been busy and that we'd schedule another meeting right away. She subsequently scheduled a meeting for this coming Thursday.

I have contacted local attorneys as well as firms in Pittsburgh and Philadelphia, who all confirm that my agreement is good. In fact, they said that it was so cut-and-dried that they offered me a reduced retainer that they said I was likely to have returned to me.

From: Charlotte Smith Andrews, VPAA
Mon 3/08/2021 6:20 PM
To: Pankhurst, Pamela
CC: W. Ways, Chair of Humanities and Social Sciences
Subject: Concerns about Fall Scheduling

Dear Pamela,

Thank you for meeting with Wily and me to discuss your fall schedule. We have placed four classes on the fall schedule for your total of 12 credit teaching hours. Any further disputes of this decision on your part will result in us placing five classes on the fall schedule for you, totaling 15 credit hours, and an expectation that you will make up for the course releases you have received for the last ten years by teaching extra classes each semester, for a total of 18 credit hours per semester, for the next ten years. Lack of cooperation on your part will be grounds for revocation of tenure and dismissal.

To reiterate: Course release actions that were made between you and my predecessor are no longer valid. I am glad that we have been able to reach clarity on several important issues. I look forward to our meeting on Monday to discuss your ideas and plans for revisioning the English and writing major.

Stay energized,

Charlotte

From: Pankhurst, Pamela
Mon 3/08/2021 6:22 PM
To: Charlotte Smith Andrews, VPAA
CC: W. Ways, Chair of Humanities and Social Sciences
Subject: Concerns about Fall Scheduling

Dear Charlotte,

I do not accept that my agreement is no longer valid, nor do the attorneys I have been consulting.

Pamela

From: Charlotte Smith Andrews, VPAA
Mon 3/08/2021 11:45 PM
To: Pankhurst, Pamela
CC: W. Ways, Chair of Humanities and Social Sciences
Subject: Concerns about Fall Scheduling

Dear Professor Pankhurst,

While we were scheduled to meet on Monday to discuss revisioning the writing major, there will be a pause on any future meetings based on your comments,

"I do not accept that my agreement is no longer valid, nor do the attorneys I have been consulting."

I will put a pause on any further communications with you—in writing or verbally—about your schedule, your students, your program, or any other matter, and put a halt on any graduation checks, textbook assistance grants, scholarships, or disability accommodations for students in your program until your attorneys provide you the consultation necessary for us to move forward positively with the work of your division and the university.

Please enjoy a rewarding weekend,

Dr. Charlotte Smith Andrews

From: Pankhurst, Pamela
Tues 3/09/2021 7:00 AM
To: The Office of President Elaine J. Moto-Lenovo
Subject: Legal Concerns

Dear Dr. Moto-Lenovo,

I am concerned about the violation of a legal agreement that I made with the previous administration. In addition to refusing to honor the agreement, Dr. Smith Andrews has made threats about my future employment, limited services to students in my program, and forbidden me from contacting the dean's office in any capacity. I need to make an appointment with you to resolve this asap.

Pamela

From: Charlotte Smith Andrews, VPAA
Tues 3/09/2021 11:00 PM
To: Faculty
CC: The Office of President Elaine J. Moto-Lenovo
Subject: Miss Millhouse

Dear Faculty,

I'm pleased to inform you that administrative assistant Kinsey Millhouse will be leaving us for other exciting opportunities in the academic enterprise.

Remain energized!

Charlotte

From: Charlotte Smith Andrews, VPAA
Wed 3/10/2021 2:00 AM
To: Faculty
CC: The Office of President Elaine J. Moto-Lenovo
Subject: Dr. Zuckerman

Dear Faculty,

I'm pleased to inform you that Dr. Wilbur Zuckerman will be leaving us for other exciting opportunities in the academic enterprise.

Remain energized!

Charlotte

From: Charlotte Smith Andrews, VPAA
Wed 3/10/2021 2:30 AM
To: Faculty
CC: The Office of President Elaine J. Moto-Lenovo
Subject: Dr. Revers-Arden

Dear Faculty,

I'm pleased to inform you that Dr. Alma Revers-Arden will be leaving us for other exciting opportunities in the academic enterprise.

Remain energized!

Charlotte

From: Charlotte Smith Andrews, VPAA
Wed 3/10/2021 2:35 AM
To: Faculty
CC: The Office of President Elaine J. Moto-Lenovo
Subject: Dr. Francie Nolen

Dear Faculty,

I'm pleased to inform you that Dr. Francie Nolen has stepped down as chair of the division of Mathematical, Physical, and Life Sciences to pursue other exciting opportunities in the academic enterprise. We are pleased that after a university-wide search for a faculty member qualified and willing to take on this responsibility, we have appointed Dr. Obi Abubakar, professor of theater, as the acting chair of the division of Mathematical, Physical, and Life Sciences, effective immediately. He is uniquely suited to this position, since we have cancelled all arts programs and are not sure what else to do with him.

Remain energized!

Charlotte

From: Raj Patel, Chair of the Division of BESOD
Thurs 3/11/2021 10:00 AM
To: Pankhurst, Pamela
Subject: FWD: Dr. Revers-Arden

Hey, Alma didn't leave for other exciting opportunities in the academic enterprise. It turns out that she's been admitted to the psychiatric ward at Sanford Regional Medical Center.

From: Pankhurst, Pamela
Thurs 3/11/2021 10:15 AM
To: Raj Patel, Chair of the Division of BESOD
Subject: FWD: Dr. Revers-Arden

OMG. Was it a suicide attempt?

From: Raj Patel, Chair of the Division of BESOD
Thurs 3/11/2021 10:20 AM
To: Pankhurst, Pamela
Subject: FWD: Dr. Revers-Arden

All I heard was that she started walking in backward circles after a Zoom meeting with Charlotte. Around and around and around in backward circles for hours on end. Bobby said he couldn't get her to stop.

From: Pankhurst, Pamela
Thurs 3/11/2021 10:25 AM
To: Raj Patel, Chair of the Division of BESOD
Subject: FWD: Dr. Revers-Arden

OMG. We've got to do something! Not only have they canceled all foreign languages and arts, our entire campus is entering a mental health crisis.

From: Raj Patel, Chair of the Division of BESOD
Thurs 3/11/2021 10:30 AM
To: Pankhurst, Pamela
Subject: FWD: Dr. Revers-Arden

But what can we do? Even tenured faculty are

dropping like flies!

From: Pankhurst, Pamela
Thurs 3/11/2021 10:35 AM
To: Raj Patel, Chair of the Division of BESOD
Subject: FWD: Dr. Revers-Arden

At least tenured faculty have some protection. We have got to organize a meeting.

From: pp@gmail.com
Thurs 3/11/2021 10:45 AM
To: bb@gmail.com
Subject: Meeting

Hi Buck,

Whatever happened to the plan for tenured faculty to meet? Since it's still snowing out, can we organize a meeting on a non-University Zoom account? I think this is getting sort of urgent. What do you think?

Pamela

From: bb@gmail.com
Thurs 3/11/2021 11:00 AM
To: tenuredfaculty@gmail.com
Subject: Meeting

It is urgently imperative for disequalibrized faculty to actionalize our concerns! Please join us in a private nonrecordable Zoom meeting on Saturday 3/13 at 9:00 PM. See the link below.

Pamela's Saved Zoom Chat Record: Meeting 3/13/2021

From Me to Raj (privately):
Did Buck just say something about archectonically epistemological hierarchies?

From Raj to All Participants:
What's Buck's favorite drink?
Gin and architectonic!

From Raj to All Participants:
What do Buck's building designers drink?
Architectonic!

From Raj to All Participants:
What does Buck do on vacation?
Takes the architectonic waters!

From Raj to All Participants:
What does Buck use to make his head shiny?
Hair architectonic!

From Me to Raj (privately):
Raj, you're losing it. Also, turn off your mic. I can hear you humming.

From Raj to Me (privately):
Turn off your camera! I can see your foot jiggling!

What does Buck do after drinking too much architectonic?

He epistomolots!

From Me to Raj (privately):
That doesn't even make sense.

From Wily to All Participants:
Charlotte told me I was incompetent.

From Jon to All Participants:
Me too!

From Me to All Participants:
Is there anyone she hasn't accused of incompetence?

From Raj to All Participants:
She threatened Francie with disciplinary action if she allowed "too many students to graduate."

From Francie Nolen to All Participants:
Not only that, she told me that there are job openings at McDonald's that I'd be better suited for!

From Obi to All Participants:
She said she doesn't understand my accent!

From Usman to All Participants:
Me too!

From Jeo-Yun to All Participants:
Me too!

From Ralph to All Participants:
She said I was lazy.

From All Participants to All Participants:
Me too!

Me too!
Me too!
Me too!
Me too!
Me too!
Me too!
Me too!

From Me to All Participants:
She called me belligerent.

From Walter to All Participants:
She called Bessie duplicitous.

From Wily to All Participants:
She threatened me with disciplinary action if I didn't skip my mother's funeral and come to a Friday afternoon meeting at 5:00 PM.

From Me to All Participants:
She threatened to revoke my tenure if I insist on having a contractual agreement upheld.

From Ralph to All Participants:
She said she was shutting down all of our majors.

From Wily to All Participants:
She said she was shutting down all of the search committees and making all of the new hires without faculty input, since we're all incompetent!

From Me to All Participants:
OMG!

From Jon to All Participants:
&*(*&**&)#$@%

From Ralph to All Participants:
I'm retiring!

From Obi to All Participants:
Everyone in our division is looking for another job.

From Wily to All Participants:
Some of them say they're going to quit with or without another job.

From Jeo-Yun to All Participants:
Mental health and morale is at an all-time low!

From Usman to All Participants:
And Elaine Moto-Lenovo keeps saying it's because of the pandemic! Not because of her toxic vice president!

From Raj to All Participants:
I CAN'T EVEN!

CONFIDENTIAL MINUTES of private meeting by Faculty Senate Secretary Ralph S. Maus (DO NOT SHARE WITH ANYONE!!!!)

We met at 9:00 PM on Saturday, March 13 on Buck's private Zoom Account. The meeting started promptly at the designated time.

Buck opened by stating that we have reached a kairotic moment and must retrench our teleological spaces.

Raj launched a diatribe against Buck, yelling at him to STOP USING BIG WORDS that no one can understand. He said, "You are what's wrong with America! You are why people think that academia is full of wimpy whiners! STOP with the architectonic epistemological poppycock bunkum! Talk like a NORMAL PERSON!"

The squares around everyone lit up as fragments of speech hurled through cyberspace, mostly designed to chastise Raj.

Finally Pamela said, "Everyone stop talking! Raj is the mildest-mannered person there is. If he is this agitated, we are in very bad shape."

Silence overtook the Zoom Room as faces turned glum. Then once again everyone started yelling at once so Buck directed them to put their grievances in the Chat.

"It's like she's programmed to disagree with everything you say," Wily said. "In a meeting the other day, I said to her, 'nice weather,' and she said, 'I think it's overly cloudy.' I said, "Well, yes, it's warm but a bit gloomy,' and she replied, 'I find this weather exceptionally cheerful and positively invigorating.' It's like you can never say anything right!"

The tenured professors agreed that our first plan of action is to make sure that President Moto-Lenovo is aware of the situation. Buck is going to issue an anonymous morale survey to all faculty so that we can gather information. We will approach President Moto-Lenovo with the results. Other next steps might be approaching the Board of Trustees and/or casting a vote of no confidence against our administration.

From: Pankhurst, Pamela
Mon 3/15/2021 6:20 PM
To: W. Ways, Chair of Humanities and Social Sciences
Subject: Recap

Hi Wily,

I just met with President Moto-Lenovo, who consulted with a lawyer who told her that my agreement was good. She said, though, that she's concerned about equity. She said that it isn't right for a female employee to benefit from an advantage not extended to male employees, even though I'm the only employee who has been asked to write an annual 30-page report detailing what I've done to earn my release. So rather than explicitly choosing to honor my agreement, she instead awarded a 3/3 load to all full professors for AY 2021-22.

But though that would reduce my courseload to 1/1 as chair, she felt that it is in the best interests of the division for me not to assume that position since she doesn't think I'm familiar enough with the other disciplines in my division. I think that's stupid since Obi is chair of a division completely outside of his expertise, but you know what? I just don't care. I am no longer willing to do the job.

Pamela

From: Charlotte Smith Andrews, VPAA
Fri 3/19/2021 6:20 PM
To: Pankhurst, Pamela
CC: The Office of President Elaine J. Moto-Lenovo
Subject: Course release

Dear Pamela,

Congratulations on your course release. Please let me know if I can support you in any way.

Remain energized,

Charlotte

From: Pankhurst, Pamela
Fri 3/19/2021 6:21 PM
To: Charlotte Smith Andrews, VPAA
CC: The Office of President Elaine J. Moto-Lenovo
Subject: Course release

Dear Charlotte,

Thanks, and I look forward to our continued work together.

Pamela

From: Charlotte Smith Andrews, VPAA
Fri 3/19/2021 6:30 PM
To: Pankhurst, Pamela
CC: Office of President Elaine J. Moto-Lenovo
Subject: Course release

Dear Pamela,

I too am looking forward to accelerating the important work in the Division of Humanities and Social Sciences.

Remain energized,

Charlotte

From: Pankhurst, Pamela
Fri 3/19/2021 6:35 PM
To: Charlotte Smith Andrews, VPAA
CC: The Office of President Elaine J. Moto-Lenovo
Subject: Course release

Dear Charlotte,

Oh, I am looking very forward to that.

Pamela

From: Charlotte Smith Andrews, VPAA
Fri 3/19/2021 6:40 PM
To: Pankhurst, Pamela
CC: Office of President Elaine J. Moto-Lenovo
Subject:: Course release

Dear Pamela,

I am looking even more forward to that than you are.

Charlotte

From: Pankhurst, Pamela
Fri 3/19/2021 6:45 PM
To: Raj Patel, Chair of the Division of BESOD
Subject: FWD: Course release

Isn't this weird? It's like she's been commanded to respond to every single e-mail I send. This could go on for hours.

From: Obi Abubakar, Chair of Mathematical, Physical, and Life Sciences
Wed 3/24/2021 12:30 PM
To: Faculty
Subject: Spring Theater Department Production

Please log on to Zoom for performances Friday and Saturday night or the Sunday matinee of our spring student theater production, "Mendel and his Peas: A One Act Play." Dr. Moto-Lenovo will make a special appearance as a deranged gun-toting nun determined to take credit for Mendel's magnificent achievements.

From: Charlotte Smith Andrews, VPAA
Thurs 3/25/2021 2:30 AM
To: Faculty
CC: The Office of President Elaine J. Moto-Lenovo
Subject: Division of Humanities and Social Sciences Chair

I am pleased to inform you that the new chair of the Division of Humanities and Social Sciences will be Mr. Bart Crocker. You all know Bart as the head of Dining and Auxiliary Services at SLAC. His extensive experience with creating balanced meals, supervising chefs, servers, and cashiers, reserving rooms around campus for events, and booking and overseeing annual events on campus such as the citywide antique car show, the summer Zombie Apocalypse Simulation camp for area schoolchildren, and the nationally recognized Cow Chip Baseball Championship League games.

I have confidence that Bart's unique experience will revive enrollment in your majors and encourage you to liven up dull academic offerings. Please prepare your annual self-evaluation and submit it to Bart by the beginning of May since he will be conducting reviews of the performance of all faculty in your division.

From: Pankhurst, Pamela
Thurs 3/25/2021 10:30 AM
To: Raj Patel, Chair of the Division of BESOD
Subject: FWD: Division of Humanities and Social Sciences Chair

OMG

...

April 2021
Professor Pamela Pankhurst To-Do List

- Call CVS and renew anxiety meds prescription
- Meeting on supporting Bobby Arden and Alma Revers-Arden through mental health and

financial crisis
- Create incentives for students to turn on cameras
- Final exams
- Turn in Accreditation Portfolio
- Get second vaccination!
- Give away extra rolls of toilet paper!
- Visit from Clarissa!

Inescape Accreditation Standard #4

4.0 The program enables the candidate to acquire and demonstrate the dispositions and capacities needed to
    4.1 Prove that God exists
    4.2 Prove that God is dead
    4.3 Leap buildings in a single bound

Grease, Sr.
Alternate Title: *Rogaine*
Snail-Paced Land Yacht, performed by Danny and his crew to the tune of "Greased Lightning"

(Danny:)

Why, this car is fuel efficient

It's preconditioned

It's a practical acquisition

It's a snail-paced land yacht

(Danny and chorus)

We'll get some adaptive cruise control and interior versatility, oh yeah

(I already own it, don't need to take a loan on it)

It's got all-wheel drive, you ladies have arrived,

You know that ain't no joke, I'll impress all the folks

Snail's Gallop! Land yachting!

Slow slow slow slow slow slow

Too tired these days to hustle, we'll take it slow and guzzle

Snail-paced land yacht! Snail-paced land yacht!

From: Pankhurst, Pamela
Mon 4/05/2021 11:42 AM
To: Harris, Kaitlyn D.
Subject: Your poems

Kaitlyn,

Attached are your most recent marked-up poems about your Isabella tiger moth. I particularly like the ambition of your combined acrostic and sestina, the poem you refer to as an acrostina. The sonnet/haiku mashup doesn't quite work for me, though. The sonku with its fourteen lines that alternate between a five-seven-five syllabic count does seem marginally more successful to me than the haikut with three lines in which each syllable is part of the rhyme scheme ababcdcdefefgg.

Dr. Pankhurst

P.S. I agree that your roommate should not be allowed to adopt an emotional support parasitic wasp, and for more reasons than the fact that they eat tiger moths. Let me know if I need to write Mr. Wilson a note advocating for you.

From: Pankhurst, Pamela
Tues 4/6/2021 12:01 PM
To: Raj Patel, Chair of the Division of BESOD
Subject: Tasks to assist Bobby and Alma

So, I offered to cancel their Filmflix subscription to help their finances while Alma is institutionalized. What did you agree to do?

And do you know what became of the Morale Survey? We filled it out weeks ago.

Transcript of Conversation between Pamela Pankhurst and Filmflix Bot

From: Filmflix <info@mailer.filmflix.com>
Sent: Saturday, April 10, 2021 11:07 AM
To: Pankhurst, Pamela
Subject: Your recent chat transcript

Hello,

Thank you for contacting Filmflix customer support.

Here is the transcript from your recent chat.

You
I need to cancel a subscription for someone who is currently incapacitated.

Josephine Filmflix
I am sorry to hear of your loss. Let me check this for you. Can you please provide the email associated with the account?

You
The e-mail is ara@slac.edu. The account number is 12345678. The phone number is 555-1206.

Josephine Filmflix
I am unable to pull up an account using that information.

You
Well then how do I do it? I have her social security number, birthdate, account number, phone number—what more could you need?

Josephine Filmflix
Do you have her twitter handle?

You
Why would I have her twitter handle?

Josephine Filmflix
Let's try another way. Can you give me her library card number?

You
Why would either of us have her library card number?

You
Can I speak to a supervisor?

Josephine Filmflix
Just to set proper expectations even my supervisor cannot do something on this since we cannot pull up an account on our end and we are using the same tools.

You
Please refer me to a supervisor.

Josephine Filmflix
Please stay connected while I check for an available one.

Josephine Filmflix
Still checking for an available supervisor.

Clive Filmflix
Hi I am Clive, a supervisor at Filmflix. Allow me to assist you further.

You
I need to cancel a subscription for someone who is currently incapacitated.

Clive Filmflix
I am sorry to hear of your loss. Let me check this for you. Can you please provide the email associated

with the account?

You

The e-mail is ara@slac.edu. The account number is 12345678. The phone number is 555-1206.

Clive Filmflix

I am unable to pull up an account using that information.

You

Well then how do I do it? I have her social security number, birthdate, account number, phone number—what more could you need?

Clive Filmflix

Do you have the customer code from her most recent Lands End catalogue?

You

I already went through all of this with Josephine. Why would I have some number from her Lands End catalogue?

Clive Filmflix

Let's try another way. Can you give me the title of the first 45 record that she ever bought?

You

Are you all robots, or what? You just keep repeating the same stuff. Why would I have any idea whether she ever bought anything on vinyl or what it was?

Clive Filmflix
We can actually help you but for us to do that, we have to locate the account first for us to make the necessary changes.

Do you still have access to her Filmflix account? Like her Filmflix is still currently logged in to a device that you have there.

You
How could her account possibly be logged in to my devices?

Clive Filmflix
In all honesty, I can help you cancel and give you a refund however, the problem here is that we are unable to locate the account so we will not be able to do that.

You
So you have no way to locate a customer? If I die tomorrow, you will continue to bill me?

Clive Filmflix
To be honest yes. We will not be able to locate the account since we really need the information that I asked earlier.

You
So in other words you will continue to gouge her bank account as long as it exists.

Clive Filmflix
Please don't think that we are not willing to help. I

mentioned earlier that we can actually help you with the request. However, it's just that we are unable to locate the account so I cannot process anything here.

You
You all are just robots with no imagination. Goodbye.

From: Pankhurst, Pamela
Sat 4/10/2021 1:00 PM
To: Raj Patel, Chair of the Division of BESOD
Subject: Tasks to assist Bobby and Alma

Well, I give up. Talking to that bot at Filmflix was like watching Alma go around and around in backward circles. It was like talking to Charlotte.

OMG Raj. I felt the exact same sense of frustration as when I talk to Charlotte. What does that mean?

From: Baker, Buck
Mon 4/12/2021 3:00 PM
To: Faculty
Subject: Morale survey results

Please find attached the results to the morale survey.

From: Raj Patel, Chair of the Division of BESOD
Mon 4/12/2021 6:00 PM
To: Pankhurst, Pamela
Subject: Morale survey results

OMG. Did you see those? I read them three times.

From: Pankhurst, Pamela
Mon 4/12/2021 6:15 PM
To: Raj Patel, Chair of the Division of BESOD
Subject: Morale survey results

There was a 95 percent response rate. We're usually lucky to get a 20 percent response rate. I copied the results into a word cloud generator and here's what I got:

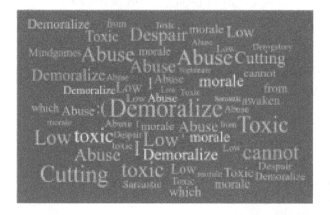

Now what do we do? We need to do something, but everyone's backing out. They're afraid they're going to lose their jobs.

From: Raj Patel, Chair of the Division of BESOD
Mon 4/12/2021 8:00 PM
To: Pankhurst, Pamela
Subject: Morale Survey Results

Unbelievable. Isn't it bizarre, how someone we've never even met can wreak so much havoc from behind a computer?

From: The Office of President Elaine J. Moto-Lenovo
Tues 4/13/2021 2:00 PM
To: Faculty
CC: Charlotte Smith Andrews, VPAA
Subject: New faculty

I am pleased to announce the results of our faculty searches. You will have the opportunity to welcome the following new hires, who will all be teaching online, at the beginning of the next academic year. They are:

- Winkie Zen, assistant professor of Dark Tourism
- Homer Karaoke, assistant professor of Cannabis Cultivation
- Pluto Lo Lomabot, instructor of Bakery Science
- Odette Drizzle, visiting assistant professor of Floral Management
- Pyramid Panhellenic, assistant professor of Viticulture and Enology
- Quartz Pumpaboo, visiting assistant professor of Badassery
- Franky Automator, assistant professor of Scientology
- Alpha Tango, instructor of Bowling and Lifeguarding
- Beep Boop, assistant professor of Miscellaneous Studies

From: pp@gmail.com
Tues 4/13/2021 6:00 PM
To: rp@gmail.com
Subject: FWD: New Faculty

OMG these are all bot names!

From: rp@gmail.com
Tues 4/13/2021 6:05 PM
To: pp@gmail.com
Subject: FWD: New Faculty

You are really fixated on this bot thing.

From: pp@gmail.com
Tues 4/13/2021 6:15 PM
To: rp@gmail.com
　　bb@gmail.com
Subject: FWD: new faculty

Raj! Buck! You guys, I know this sounds insane, but I think that Elaine is hiring bots in place of professors. And what if Charlotte is actually a bot. Doesn't that make sense? Think about it. Doesn't she troll everybody? And doesn't she look like an avatar when she's on camera?

From: bb@gmail.com
Tues 4/13/2021 7:00 PM
To: rp@gmail.com
　　pp@gmail.com
Subject: FWD: new faculty

Ha ha, that's remarkably comical!

From: rp@gmail.com
Tues 4/13/2021 7:30 PM
To: bb@gmail.com
　　pp@gmail.com
Subject: FWD: new faculty

Not to mention really funny!

From: pp@gmail.com
Tues 4/13/2021 7:35 PM
To: rp@gmail.com
　bb@gmail.com
Subject: FWD: new faculty

I know it sounds totally insane, but I am serious.

From: bb@gmail.com
Wed 4/14/2021 7:00 PM
To: rp@gmail.com
　pp@gmail.com
Subject: FWD: new faculty

So, I've been ruminating over Pamela's speculative witticism and it occurs to me that the Board of Trustees did recently praise President Moto-Lenovo's budget decisions. She apparently has saved a few million dollars on salaries alone.

From: rp@gmail.com
Wed 4/14/2021 7:30 PM
To: bb@gmail.com
　pp@gmail.com
Subject: FWD: new faculty

That's just because everyone is quitting.

From: pp@gmail.com
Wed 4/14/2021 7:35 PM
To: rp@gmail.com
　bb@gmail.com
Subject: FWD: new faculty

No, it's because President Moto-Lenovo is hiring bots!

From: rp@gmail.com
Wed 4/14/2021 8:30 PM
To: bb@gmail.com
   pp@gmail.com
Subject: FWD: new faculty

You're not going to commence walking around and around in backward circles like Alma, are you?

From: bb@gmail.com
Wed 4/14/2021 8:45 PM
To: rp@gmail.com
   pp@gmail.com
Subject: FWD: new faculty

How is Alma, by the way?

From: rp@gmail.com
Wed 4/14/2021 9:00 PM
To: bb@gmail.com
   pp@gmail.com
Subject: FWD: new faculty

I heard she's been sedated and is mostly walking sideways. There's no consistent forward movement, but it's still progress.

From: pp@gmail.com
Wed 4/14/2021 9:05 PM
To: rp@gmail.com
   bb@gmail.com
Subject: FWD: new faculty

You guys! Focus! We have got to do something about this!

From: Craig, Brittany
Wed 4/14/2021 9:15 PM
To: Pankhurst, Pamela
Poetry Class
Subject: my final poem

Hey Mrs. Pankhurst and Everyone,

I'm sending the final poem in my project for your feedback before I turn in my portfolio tomorrow morning. Content warning: this haiku contains themes of abuse, suicide, mental illness, and violence, and might be triggering. Please don't feel like you have to read it if you think it might upset you.

Mean mean mean mean mean
Anger anger anger ang
Er sad sad sad sad

From: bb@gmail.com
Wed 4/14/2021 9:30 PM
To: rp@gmail.com
pp@gmail.com
Subject: FWD: new faculty

Charlotte presents like a human being. I don't know how you'd compel a bot to articulate some of these utterances. I'm going to bed, vis a vis obtaining vital rest. Let's revisit this tomorrow.

From: pp@gmail.com
Thurs 4/15/2021 1:00 PM
To: rp@gmail.com
    bb@gmail.com
Subject: FWD: new faculty

Take a look at these. They're from Chatbot sites:

"In addition to having the capacity to answer basic questions per a pre-loaded script, our bot is geared to automate conversations and appear authentic, as if the answers were being provided via a live human interaction. . . More than just chatbots, it's conversational AI."

"Create sophisticated automated conversations with our comprehensive and intuitive interface."

"Using artificial intelligence and natural language processing, our advanced lifelike chatbot can simulate face-to-face conversation with users. Natural language processing (NLP) makes it possible for your bot to read text, hear and interpret speech, measure sentiment and purpose, and simulate human speech using natural lifelike speech rhythms and patterns."

From: bb@gmail.com
Thurs 4/15/2021 6:00 PM
To: rp@gmail.com
    pp@gmail.com
Subject: FWD: new faculty

OK, I'll concur that sometimes Charlotte seems a little robotic. But even if your theory had a modicum of credence, how would we possibly corroborate it?

From: pp@gmail.com
Thurs 4/15/2021 9:00 PM
To: rp@gmail.com
   bb@gmail.com
Subject: HELP!!!!

So you guys, things are getting really weird and scary! I was talking to Clarissa on the phone in my living room just now. Without going into too much detail about my love life, Clarissa had asked me if I felt the same way about all my exes as I did about her, and I said, "All exes?" And all of a sudden the blue light started swirling at the top of my Alexa. Here is the transcript of my Amazon Echo History from that point on:

On 4/15/2021 08:00 PM on Pamela's Echo
Alexa: "I do not understand this request"

Pamela: "I wasn't talking to you, Alexa. I was talking to Clarissa."

On 4/15/2021 08:00 PM on Pamela's Echo
Alexa: "I do not understand this request"

On 4/15/2021 08:00 PM on Pamela's Echo

Pamela: "I said 'all exes,' not 'Alexa.' I was telling Clarissa that I don't feel the same way about her as my other exes. Oh, never mind."

On 4/15/2021 08:01 PM on Pamela's Echo
Alexa: "Pamela, you do not need to be so belligerent just

because you are incompetent."

On 4/15/2021 08:01 PM on Pamela's Echo
Alexa: "Pamela, maybe you are becoming irrelevant and should quit your job. Would you like me to access your retirement accounts?"

On 4/15/2021 08:02 PM on Pamela's Echo

So that totally freaked me out and I yanked the Echo's cord out of the wall and escaped upstairs to talk to Clarissa. Here's my Siri history from that moment on:

Pamela's Siri History

4/15/2021 8:03 PM on Pamela's iPhone

Pamela: "Hey, seriously spooky, Clarissa! I moved upstairs so Alexa can't hear me!

Siri: *Sorry, I missed that. Could you say it again please?*

Pamela: "Oh my God, I'm not talking to you, Siri. I'm just trying to have a phone conversation with Clarissa!"

Siri: *Maybe you could get your point across if you weren't so incompetent.*

Pamela: "I've got to get off the phone, Clarissa. This is creepy. I'm going to leave the phone in the bathroom and I'll e-mail you from my home office."

Siri: *Sorry, I missed that. Could you say it again please? Also, you are incompetent. You don't do it right. Everything you do is the wrong way. Incompetent incompetent incompetent. Maybe you should quit your job and let someone more competent take over.*

I hastily said goodbye to Clarissa and powered off my iPhone. But now I was really losing it. I wasn't sure if I'd gone off the deep end and was imagining all of this, so I went to my computer and printed out the above transcripts. Then I tried to log onto my e-mail, but I was immediately prompted to change my password. Except the security questions that came up weren't my usual security questions, and the answers were already filled in! Here's a screenshot:

PAMELA PANKHURST
E-MAIL PASSWORD RESET
Answer the following security questions:

Charlotte Smith Andrews says that you are:
incompetent

Charlotte Smith Andrews knows that you are also
belligerent

You may have thought what you did in the past works but it
doesn't

In the Captcha below, identify pictures with stoplights, crosswalks, or buses that resemble Charlotte Smith Andrews' eyebrows:

At this point, I powered off the computer and went

downstairs. My heart was pounding so hard I could barely think. I turned on the TV to try to distract myself with a movie but was immediately taken to the Hulu Password Reset screen; I turned on my phone briefly to take a quick photo and write this e-mail. The photo is attached:

HULU PASSWORD RESET
Answer the following security questions:

I, YOUR NAME HERE, hereby resign from my job at Sanford Liberal Arts College. I have severely mismanaged my program, do not know the correct way to teach my classes, and have become incompetent and irrelevant. I understand that my resignation and my exit from a field that Charlotte Smith Andrews knows far better than I do is in everyone's best interests.

I unplugged the TV and am trying to get this written as fast as possible because texts have started dinging in again telling me how incompetent I am. You guys, I have a plan but I need your help. We can orchestrate it so that if I'm wrong or if I get caught, you guys won't be implicated. Can we convene a top secret meeting on Raj and Saanvi's porch to discuss this?

Oh my god somebody's ringing my doorbell! My phone is beeping with texts that keep buzzing through to my Apple watch. Alexa and Siri are yelling at the top of their lungs even though I unplugged Alexa and turned off my phone! My car audio system is lighting up in the driveway! My TV screen is flashing with threatening messages! My computer browser history tab has opened without me touching it and my cursor is moving around on its own. Multiple new tabs keep opening! I'm getting confirmation e-mails saying that I've bought hundreds of dollars worth of video games, and a confirmation e-mail about a new account created, and an e-mail from the credit card company detecting fraudulent charges!

I know it'll sound like I'm bonkers and just making all of this up, but I couldn't possibly have manufactured all of this evidence. She's in all of my devices! SHE'S IN MY HEAD!!!! Someone come get me! I'm going to sneak out the back door. I'll meet you at the corner. Raj, can I stay with you and Saanvi for a few days? Hurry!

From: Pankhurst, Pamela
Fri 4/16/2021 8:00 AM
To: Office of President Elaine J. Moto-Lenovo
CC: Baker, Buck
    Raj Patel, Chair of the Division of BESOD
Subject: Morale Survey

Dear President Moto-Lenovo,

The morale survey results are in, and we have significant concerns. We'd like to meet with you to discuss them. Due to the highly confidential nature of this information along with the fact that we are now all fully vaccinated, we'd like to meet with you in person. Would it be possible to arrange a time? This is urgent.

Thank you.

Pamela, Raj, and Buck

From: The Office of President Elaine J. Moto-Lenovo
Mon 4/16/2021 9:00 PM
To: Pankhurst, Pamela; Raj Patel, Chair of the Division of BESOD; Baker, Buck; O'Harrell, Scarlett
Subject: Morale Survey

Scarlett, can you please set up a meeting with Professors Pankhurst, Patel, and Baker?

...

May 2021
Professor Pamela Pankhurst To-Do List

- Get anxiety meds refilled
- Ask for stronger dose
- Read books
- Tend campfire
- Send Saanvi for groceries
- Meet with investigator

Things To Do When I Return to Civilization:

- Hire lawyer?
- Clean out office?
- Check retirement accounts?
- Check on COBRA benefits?
- Look for another job?
- Sell my house?
- Clarissa?

From: Heidi Spyri, Dombey and Dombey, Higher Education Law and Services
Mon 5/17/2021 2:00 PM
To: Board of Trustees, Sanford Liberal Arts College
Subject: Investigation

After extensive interviews with participating parties, we have reached our conclusions regarding our investigation of recent ethical violations that escalated to an alleged murder attempt at Sanford Liberal Arts College.

In an interview, Professor Pamela Pankhurst, director of the English and writing program, stated that she; Professor Buck Baker, President of the Faculty Senate; and Raj Patel, Chair of Business administration, Education, Sports-related careers, and Other miscellaneous fields that Don't fit anywhere else, made an appointment with President Elaine J. Moto-Lenovo for Tuesday, April 20 at 3:00 PM to discuss a faculty morale survey that had been issued by the faculty senate.

At 2:58 p.m., Professor Pankhurst was the first to arrive at President Moto-Lenovo's office on the second floor of the administration building, which was largely deserted due to the fact that most staff members were still working from home as a result of Covid 19. Pankhurst and Moto-Lenovo located themselves in couches and chairs at the south end of the president's office and exchanged pleasantries while waiting for Professors Baker and Patel.

At 3:05, Pankhurst reported, Patel and Baker rushed

into the room, urging Moto-Lenovo to accompany them to Wortz Hall to deal with an emergency situation. A parent, it seemed, had locked himself in the elevator and was threatening to blow up the building if his child wasn't allowed to graduate. The student had been denied graduation after the university refused to allow his Red Cross training to be substituted for a canceled campus lifeguarding course.

Despite the parent's bomb threat, no campus police had been alerted. When Moto-Lenovo moved toward her phone to contact them, Baker stopped her, explaining, "The parent threatened to detonate explosives in the event of intervention by law enforcement individuals."

"He demanded to talk to the president of the university," Patel added.

"Guardlifing?" Moto-Lenovo reportedly said as she dropped the phone receiver back into its cradle and rushed out of her office with Patel, who was not, it should be noted, engaged in his characteristic humming and Baker, who was, it should also be noted, lugging with him a very large book which he admitted that he always carries on his person.

Left alone in the presidential suite, Professor Pankhurst admitted to attempting unauthorized computer access, tapping random passwords into Moto-Lenovo's system. After trying combinations like 123456 and 654321, Pankhurst noticed a sticky note that read "Password" on the wall next to the computer. The word "Password" yielded no results. Inspired by speech patterns that she had noted, Pankhurst typed, instead, "Wordpass."

At approximately 3:15 PM, Pankhurst officially became an illegal hacker, breaking into President Moto-Lenovo's e-mail account.

•

Professors Baker and Patel reported that, during this same time period, they led President Moto-Lenovo down the stairs and out the door of the administration building. They subsequently halted on the sidewalk, cautioning her that they needed to make a plan for approaching the unhinged parent.

The three conferred for five minutes outside of Wortz Hall, Professor Baker stalling their progress by using an average of twenty words whenever two would have sufficed.

Finally, having exhausted Moto-Lenovo's patience but not Baker's vocabulary, the trio entered the largely deserted building, donning masks and scanning their IDs according to official Covid protocol. Professors Baker and Patel kept fumbling theirs and accidentally scanning them backward, resulting in a two-minute delay.

•

Meanwhile, in the building next door, Pankhurst skimmed the titles of Moto-Lenovo's Outlook files, clicking into her sent mailbox and glancing through it. She confessed that she was hoping to identify the name of a company that specialized in academic artificial intelligence, but was slowed by a pounding heart and quivering fingers and the realization that she had forgotten her bifocals.

Pankhurst began to type words like "robot," "AI," "chatbot," and "deanbot" into the box. None yielded any results.

She jumped when she heard a door slam in the hall. Rapidly she logged out of the computer, snatched the e-mail from the printer, and raced to seat herself on the couch.

Detecting only silence, she crept to the office doorway and found that a sudden wind through an open window had caused a door to slam. After confirming that she was still alone in the presidential suite, Professor Pankhurst compounded hacking charges against her by relogging on to President Moto-Lenovo's computer.

•

At approximately 3:25 PM in Wortz Hall, both Patel and Baker confirmed in independent interviews, the president and the two professors approached the closed elevator that had halted on the first floor. The three university employees commenced to yell at the elevator doors for approximately six minutes.

While memories of their actual words were only partial, Patel reportedly yelled at the elevator, "Mr.

Kazminski, are you there? We have brought the president to talk to you. We have not called the police, just as you asked."

Baker allegedly yelled at the elevator, "Please do not detonate your explosive! We have summoned administrative officials with extensive epistemological authority in the architectonicality of the higher education endeavor to negotiate with you!"

At their encouragement, President Moto-Lenovo joined in, yelling at the elevator, "Mr. Kazminski, I am sure we can work out some way for your son to get credit for guard lifing and graduate! Please just come out of the elevator and let's talk!"

Then, at approximately 3:31 PM, the elevator whirred as the light showed it rising to the second floor.

Patel later described feeling a prickly sense that something wasn't quite right as he exclaimed, "He's headed upstairs!" He, Baker, and Moto-Lenovo went racing for the stairs to intercept the bomb threatener.

•

Back at the presidential office suite, Professor Pankhurst resumed her search through President Moto-Lenovo's e-mail, failing to unearth any incriminating information. Nevertheless, she persisted, trying words and combinations that resulted in the response, "We didn't find anything.

Try a different keyword."

By now, sweat was pouring down Pankhurst's sides and trickling along her sternum. Her hands were trembling so hard that she couldn't type without having to constantly backtrack to correct typos. In answer, the screen flashed,

We didn't find anything. Try a different keyword.

We didn't find anything. Try a different keyword.

We didn't find anything. Try a different keyword.

•

At 3:33 PM in Wortz Hall, Patel, Baker, and Moto-Lenovo reached the top of the stairs, at which point Patel stumbled and fell.

"Ouch, wait, help!" he said, moaning, groaning, and clutching his ankle.

Baker paused to inquire about his wellbeing, engaging in a laborious effort to assist Patel to his feet and make a prolonged examination of his capacity for walking.

Moto-Lenovo craned her neck to peer into the dark and empty upstairs hall outside of the dark and empty office of the Dean and Vice President of Academic Affairs. Then she exclaimed, "He's going to get away!" and bolted toward the hall.

"Madam, we must not let you encumber the risk of entering that passageway alone!" Baker protested, attempting to detain Moto-Lenovo, who surged on toward the elevator, ignoring him.

Exchanging a frantic glance, Baker and Patel followed her into the hall, beelining for the elevator at about 3:36 PM.

The doors, Patel reported, were open.

The elevator, Baker corroborated, was devoid of any recent or current inhabitants.

Moto-Lenovo, they both independently recounted, dashed wild-eyed into the elevator and then came out, insisting that she needed to return to her office to call campus police.

"But what if he's still in the building?" Patel asked, and set about poking his nose into doorways up and down the hall while Moto-Lenovo and Baker looked on.

•

Around 3:38, in the presidential suite, Pankhurst began to search Word documents and Excel spreadsheets, scanning titles in the hope that one would trigger inspiration. But they were, she reported, all dull: "Speech to faculty about pandemic preparedness," "Budgets for FY 2020-21," "Detailed PowerPoint on how to pinch the wire on your mask in order to keep it from slipping down your nose."

Pankhurst strained her ears for sounds in the building outside the door of the suite. She paced briefly. Then she thought, "Budgets for FY 2020-21!"

Plopping back down in Moto-Lenovo's leather swivel office chair, Pankhurst rapidly clicked open the spreadsheet. Struggling to read the tiny print with no knowledge of how to enlarge a spreadsheet, she ran her finger along the computer screen from one item to the next.

Pankhurst reported yelling aloud, "Bingo!" and then freezing in horror lest someone hear her.

Once again reassured by silence that no one was nearby, she craned her head close to the computer and deciphered the fine print to find a $500 paid subscription to a company called Bossbots.

Control P, Pankhurst typed triumphantly, and the printer came to life and began to spew more pages.

Then, abruptly, it stopped. A light flashed, indicating a printer jam.

Pankhurst rushed to the machine, pressing buttons and opening and closing doors, but the light continued flashing. Reportedly recalling a similar problem with the Wortz Hall printers, Pankhurst turned the printer off and then on again.

Waiting tensely for it to reboot, and worrying that Moto-Lenovo would claim that the budget item was for admissions chatbots, Pankhurst sagged in defeat just as, across the quad on the second floor of Wortz

Hall, Patel called Baker to a doorway.

•

"I think I found something!" Patel said, scraping up a fingertip quantity of dust, which he and Baker proceeded to study at great length.

But Moto-Lenovo did not engage. "There's nobody here," she was quoted as saying at roughly 3:40 PM. "I need to get back to my office." When she shoved her hand into her skirt pocket and then removed it rapidly, Patel's attention was caught by the way the pocket sagged.
His eyes traveled from her face to her pocket as he noted a glitter in her eyes and a corresponding glint of metal concealed underneath her clothing.

Patel nudged Baker and pointed at the drooping pocket. As Moto-Lenovo turned on her heel and headed toward the stairs, Patel and Baker exchanged glances that both later described as "panicked."

Here in their follow-up interviews, both Baker and Patel capitulated and admitted to this investigator that their trip to Wortz Hall had been a ploy to lure Moto-Lenovo from her office and that they had still not received an all-clear from Pankhurst. They hastened to accompany Moto-Lenovo down the stairs and out the door, pointing out fabricated "evidence" of the bomb threatener's whereabouts, including a footprint in the dirt and a paper cup scuttling in the wind.

With nary a glance, Moto-Lenovo continued her determined stride back toward the administration building, both professors reported.

•

At 3:42 PM, the printer once again began spewing pages. Peeling her sweat-soaked shirt away from her skin, Pankhurst glanced out the window and saw Moto-Lenovo approaching the building. She knew it was only a matter of minutes before Moto-Lenovo arrived at the presidential suite.

Hastening to close out the computer's open windows, Pankhurst clicked on Moto-Lenovo's e-mail and did a quick search for Bossbots. Nothing appeared, due to the fact, Pankhurst later theorized, that the Outlook search feature "sucks."

Just as she was about to log off in defeat, another message dinged in. Pankhurst's eyes bulged as she read the message, or so she reported, though this may have been just a figure of speech, given that this investigator observed no evidence of thyroid issues or eyes protruding out of their actual sockets.

The message read as follows:

From: Bossbots, Inc.
Tues 4/20/2021 3:42 PM
To: The Office of President Elaine J. Moto-Lenovo
Subject: Your settings

Thank you for entrusting Bossbots, Inc. with all of your

administrative AI needs. We are writing to confirm your recent order of eight new Chatbots:

Winkie Zen
Homer Karaoke
Pluto Lo Lomabot
Odette Drizzle
Pyramid Panhellenic
Quartz Pumpaboo
Franky Automator
Alpha Tango
Beep Boop

Please confirm the settings on these ProfessorBots, which will all go live on August 15, 2021.

In addition, please confirm the settings on your DeanBot, "Charlotte." We have reconfigured them based on the following request:

From: *The Office of President Elaine J. Moto-Lenovo*
Tues 4/18/2021 6:00 PM
To: *Bossbots, Inc.*
Subject: *Your settings*

I am submitting an order form for the new ProfessorBots, who will be programmed to deliver lectures at intervals and grade periodic tests using ScanTron technology. We will need to promote retention by keeping them on highly supportive settings. This includes replying to pre-programmed e-mail catchwords with the following phrases:

- *"I'm so sorry you are feeling ill. Please make your*

health your priority, and do your best to keep up with the syllabus."
- *"I am so sorry that you were offended. I will alter my speech and classroom manner in any way that you request."*
- *"You are a genius. Perhaps you should apply to graduate school."*

I will provide additional instructions soon.

As for Charlotte the DeanBot, I think the algorithm needs some adjustment. It appears that we went too far toward the troll continuum and need to dial it back just a tad. It is true that we have managed to dispense with some expensive employees who can be replaced with additional Bots, but we do need to avoid lawsuits.

Thanks ever so much,

President Moto-Lenovo

Shaking triumphantly, Pankhurst pushed Control P and waited for the printer to fire up. When the printer didn't respond, she pushed Control P a second time. She logged off of the computer, grabbed a sanitizing wipe to swipe fingerprints from the keyboard and screen—further evidence of her criminal intent—and snatched papers out of the printer as they emerged one by one.

Then, once again, the printer shut down and the light began to blink. Words began to appear, scrolling across the computer screen. Blurred photos that Pankhurst shot with her camera phone show words that we have reconstructed as follows:

> *Pamela, you can't escape me this easily.*
> *You are incompetent.*
>
> *You are belligerent.*
>
> *You may have thought you were doing a good job for the last twenty years, but nothing you're doing is right.*

Frantic, Pankhurst took photos of the computer screen, the ceiling, the carpet, the corner of a drawer as she leapt up to open and slam doors on the printer, knowing that she didn't have time to reboot it.

Then, sliding open the paper drawer, she discovered the problem: it was empty. Shoving a pile of paper into the drawer, she held her breath as the printer started up again.

More words scrolled across the computer screen:

> *Why don't you just give up?*

Pankhurst clicked on the Microsoft icon and the power button, throwing the computer into sleep mode. Then, grabbing the printouts, she raced across the room and arranged herself casually on the couch, powering down her phone that had started to vibrate with incoming texts, with corresponding regular tickles to her arm as her Apple watch delivered duplicate versions of those messages:

Pamela, you can't escape me.

I'm in your head. You'll never have a moment of peace again.

Be free.

Resign.

Pankhurst was jiggling her foot madly when, at approximately 3:44 PM, the door was flung open and Moto-Lenovo entered, trailed by Patel and Baker, eyes fixed on Moto-Lenovo's pocket.

This account will be continued in another e-mail, as it is time for the investigator's Zoom fiction writing seminar.

Sincerely,

Heidi Spyri, JD, Dombey and Dombey, Higher Education Law and Services
MFA Candidate in Fiction, Spalding   University

From: Heidi Spyri, Dombey and Dombey, Higher Education Law and Services
Tues 5/18/2021 1:00 PM
To: Board of Trustees, Sanford Liberal Arts College
Subject: Investigation, continued

At the end of my last report, Moto Lenovo, Patel, and Baker had just returned to the president's office where Pankhurst had been hacking into classified information. At the moment that this account resumes, Patel had the wherewithal to surreptitiously reach into his pocket and press "record" on his cell phone. Therefore, the rest of this eyewitness testimony is backed up by a transcript of that recording, in which one can hear the printer come to life as it began to print more pages.

Suddenly, Pankhurst reported, she recalled that, in her agitation, she'd pushed Control P twice.

"What's this?" said Moto-Lenovo. One can hear the sound of quick strides and shuffling paper, presumably as President Moto-Lenovo seized the emerging printouts of her e-mail correspondence.

Pankhurst reported here that Moto-Lenovo glanced at the papers, then raised her eyes to confront Pankhurst, Patel, and Baker.

Her hand sank into her pocket.

Before she could draw her gun, Patel tackled her from behind. The ensuing scuffle is audible as Moto-Lenovo collapsed to the carpet, Pankhurst screamed, and a gun popped.

Baker staggered backward and crashed dramatically to the floor with a groan.

"You shot him!" Pankhurst exclaimed. "You shot Buck!"

Moto-Lenovo crawled forward, fumbling for the gun.

"NO," Pankhurst screamed, racing to kick the weapon out of the way.

Moto-Lenovo beat her to it, seizing the gun and leaping to her feet.

Patel came to an abrupt halt in the middle of the carpet, where he'd been edging toward Baker to check for a pulse.

Moto-Lenovo swerved to point the gun at Pankhurst before swinging it back to direct it at Patel.

"Give me all of the papers in your hand and I'll let you go," Moto-Lenovo ordered.

"Don't shoot!" Pankhurst cried out. "We don't want any trouble!"

"Just hand me the papers and we'll call an ambulance for Dr. Baker," Moto-Lenovo said. "We'll just say that he confronted me and threatened to shoot himself if I didn't fire Charlotte. I know that mental health on this campus is at an all-time low. Everyone will believe my story."

"Why are you doing this? Why are you destroying our campus?" Pamela asked. At this moment, she said later, the papers trembled so ferociously in her hands that she passed them to Patel.

"I am the best president SLAC has ever had," Moto-Lenovo said. "I have created a model for reducing employee bloat that will revolutionize the academic enterprise not just here, but nationally and internationally. Now, just give me those papers and you can go free."

All of a sudden, Patel began to hum under his breath, distracting Moto-Lenovo.

In that split second, Pankhurst abruptly moved forward, taking quick right counterclockwise circular steps in between Moto-Lenovo's feet, placing her left hand to the side of the gun and maneuvering her body to Moto-Lenovo's right.

Wrist-locking Moto-Lenovo's right hand, she gracefully shoved her to the ground.

"I did it!" Pankhurst exclaimed, pointing the gun toward Moto-Lenovo. "I performed the Aiki-Jiujitsu method of handgun disarmament! I learned it on YouTube!"

Just as Patel rushed toward the phone to call campus police, Baker stirred and heaved himself to his feet. "Buck! I thought she shot you!" Pankhurst exclaimed.

"Ha, do you know how often people try to shoot me?" Baker roared cheerfully, holding out his *Dictionary of Multisyllabic Words, Pretentious Phrases, and Impenetrable Academic Jargon*. "That's why I carry this! It's made of a mineral called boomerangium that deflects bullets!"

Baker proceeded to point out a pattern of nicks and dings left by previous murder attempts.

Moto-Lenovo rose calmly to her feet. "That's not a real gun," she told the trio. "It's a prop for my role as a gun-toting nun in 'Mendel and his Peas.' That's why you can't see any new marks on the cover of Buck's *Dictionary of Multisyllabic Words, Pretentious Phrases, and Impenetrable Academic Jargon*!"

Exclamations can be heard as they reportedly examined the book where there were, indeed, no signs of any fresh bullets.

"And guess what," Moto-Lenovo continued. "I knew what was going on all along. I'm the one who made the Wortz Hall elevator go up to the second floor with my remote control elevator app. When you hacked into my computer, Pamela, you were just letting Charlotte get a stronger hold on you. She's in your devices. She's in every device you touch. She'll follow you everywhere. It's likely that she has implanted a chip in your brain through the vaccination site on your arm. You will never be free of her."

And as if on cue, three cell phones dinged: Pankhurst's, Patel's, and Baker's.

This is Charlotte. You are all incompetent! said the texts.

You've mismanaged everything!

You don't know what you're doing!

You can't do anything right!

Why don't you give up and resign?

"We've got to go! Come on!" Pankhurst yelled.

The three high-tailed it out of the president's suite, handing off the prop gun to a campus policeman they passed on the stairs. Yelling back that they'd catch up with him later, they crashed through the administration building and across the quad to Wortz Hall.

Rustles and shouts can be heard as, in Pankhurst's office, they hastily and indiscriminately printed out e-mails and documents, Pankhurst scrolling rapidly and tapping print commands while Patel and Baker ran back and forth, retrieving and collating papers from the printer.

"This computer is getting really hot," Pankhurst said as the fan whirred and hustled to cool it down.

"Just a few more," she muttered, tapping the print command over and over.

The computer grunted and creaked. All at once, it emitted a low groan as if haunted.

"No, no, no, no, no, no," Pankhurst is heard yelling on Patel's cell phone recording, followed by a frenetic staccato of fingers meeting a keyboard, a loud moan, a few more quick clicks of keys.

"Nothing will open!" Pankhurst cried out.

Patel reported that at this moment, smoke emitted from the computer and the screen went blank.

"She got your computer!" Patel yelled. "Unplug it. Let's try mine."

The trio flew down the hall to Patel's office, accessing Pankhurst's e-mail and Dropbox, rapidly printing several more pages.

Suddenly, the computer restarted.

After waiting fifteen minutes to get back online, Pankhurst began to print again, but the computer shut down and restarted a second time.

With a flurry of profanities, Pankhurst, Patel, and Baker noisily seized the growing pile of papers and pounded off down the hall, disturbing a group of students strolling purposefully back and forth between classrooms as part of a proctor-administered final in former professor Revers-Arden's "Art of Walking" seminar.

By the time the trio reached Baker's office, texts were dinging into their cell phones at the pace of three per second, reportedly reading, in part,

You are incompetent!
Retire peacefully.
There will be real guns next time.

As Pankhurst logged into her e-mail, a new message appeared:

From: Charlotte Smith Andrews, VPAA
Tues 4/20/2021 5:00 PM
To: Emily Bronty, Gondal Literary Agency
CC: *Pankhurst, Pamela*
Subject: *Proposal for new musical, ANNIE SR.*

Many popular musicals have been issued in "junior editions" for middle school productions, but what about our senior citizens? There is a dearth of material for dramatic productions in retirement communities, assisted living facilities, nursing homes, and senior activity centers. I propose to fill that gap by recreating a series of musicals specifically directed at senior performers, musicians, producers, and audiences.

Annie Sr. will focus on a hardworking, unappreciated, misrepresented director of a nursing home, Dr. Hannigan, and her incompetent, belligerent staff who do nothing but complain about their hard-knock lives and jab her with safety pins. In the end, she triumphs, singing the musical's signature number, "Tonight":

Oh, the sun will go down, tonight
bet your firstborn child
that tonight, there'll be dark.
Just thinking about tonight,
wipes away all smiling and all laughter
and all light.
When I'm stuck with a staff
that's daft and whiny,
I just get out my gun
and shoot and run...

As the three read the computer screen, a robotic

voice emerged, singing these lyrics.

Pankhurst rapidly closed all of the open windows.

"She's making fun of me," Pankhurst said. "It's true! She's not just in my devices! She's in my head!"

"She's not making fun of you, she's threatening us! And it's not just your devices! It's systemic!" Patel said. "She's coming after us tonight. We've got to do something!"

"It's multi-systemic!" Buck corrected, snatching the last document out of the computer just as all of the computers, printers, and lights in the building went dark.

•

Screeching down streets and gunning through yellow lights, Pankhurst reportedly drove Baker, Patel, and the pile of papers to Walmart for supplies to prepare the sheaf of documents for mailing.
Then, at the do-it-yourself kiosk in the lobby of the closed post office in downtown Sanford, they weighed and affixed postage to the large padded envelope.

"This package contains evidence of the dysfunction of our campus during the last year," Pankhurst scrawled in nearly illegible handwriting before addressing the envelope to the SLAC Board of Trustees and slipping the package through the overnight slot.

Though the three had powered off their cell phones, messages continued to beep in, and agitated, still convinced that she and her colleagues were in danger, Pankhurst suggested that they should go off the grid for an unspecified period of time.

As a result, Baker, Patel, and Pankhurst made a quick plan to retreat to cabins in Allegany State Park, agreeing to gather supplies and reconvene in two hours at the park's entrance.

Pankhurst dropped the others on campus to retrieve their vehicles. Here, Patel's recording ends. Patel and Baker report that their evenings proceeded without further incident.

However, Pankhurst did not fare so well.

Here, this investigator must temporarily suspend this account in order to complete her cross-genre exploration in screenwriting for her MFA coursework.

Sincerely,

Heidi Spyri, JD, Dombey and Dombey, Higher Education Law and Services
MFA Candidate in Fiction, Spalding University

From: Heidi Spyri, Dombey and Dombey, Higher Education Law and Services
Thurs 5/20/2021 5:00 PM
To: Board of Trustees, Sanford Liberal Arts College
Subject: Investigation, part 3

In lieu of a continued official report, in the interest of time, this investigator is killing two birds with one stone by submitting her cross-genre exploration in screenwriting, which she will be pitching as a Netflix Original Series. It is a true and accurate rendering of Pamela Pankhurst's testimony.

EXT. CAR DRIVING ALONG CITY STREET—7:30 PM, AROUND DUSK

CUT TO

INT. FRONT SEAT OF CAR

PAMELA *drives down deserted streets toward her home. Glancing at the passenger seat, her eye lights on a book.*

CUT TO

Book on seat, THE DICTIONARY OF MULTISYLLABIC WORDS, PRETENTIOUS PHRASES, AND IMPENETRABLE ACADEMIC JARGON.

CUT TO

PAMELA's *face as she realizes that her colleague BUCK has left the book behind. She glances in the rearview mirror and cuts the wheel as if to turn the car around*

SIRIUS XM:

Spontaneously turning itself on

You can't escape me, Pamela.

PAMELA *jumps and visibly pales.*

DASHBOARD, WORDS SCROLLING:

Incompetent belligerent mismanagement
wrong wrong wrong

EXT. CAR PULLS INTO DRIVEWAY—7:35 PM, *dusk falling rapidly*

CUT TO

INT. FRONT SEAT OF CAR—7:35 PM, *ominously shadowy*

PAMELA *rips gearshift into park. She is trembling violently. She snatches up THE DICTIONARY OF MULTISYLLABIC WORDS, PRETENTIOUS PHRASES, AND IMPENETRABLE ACADEMIC JARGON and hugs it as she opens the car door.*

EXT. SIDE PORCH—7:36 PM, *dark closing in*

PAMELA *unlocks her back door.*

INT. TV ROOM—7:36 PM

The house is silent and the room is dark except for the glow of the 80-inch TV gifted to PAMELA *by her off-and-on-again girlfriend Clarissa. Considering it "embarrassingly large,"* PAMELA *never turns the TV off because she doesn't know how.*

CUT TO

PAMELA's APPLE WATCH and then her CELL PHONE. *They remain lifeless, appearing to be ordinary devices.*

INT. STAIRS—7:37 PM

PAMELA *creeps upstairs, head turning and eyes darting around her as if looking for signs of an intruder.*

INT. BEDROOM—7:37 and 30 seconds

PAMELA *visibly relaxes as she fills a DUFFEL BAG with clothing, toiletries, and books before heading back out of the room.*

INT. STAIRS—7:45

Lights flash off in the bedroom and then on the staircase as PAMELA *flips the switches.*

INT. KITCHEN—7:45 and 23 seconds

PAMELA *loads COLORFUL STRING BAGS FROM FRANCE with perishable and nonperishable foods.*

INT. TV ROOM—7:50

PAMELA *appears in the doorway, lugging her armload of bags and items to the back door.*

Abruptly, she is yanked off her feet.

The duffel and grocery bags spill around her and THE DICTIONARY OF MULTISYLLABIC WORDS, PRETENTIOUS PHRASES, AND IMPENETRABLE ACADEMIC JARGON falls onto her foot, fracturing a bone just as she topples to the floor hard enough to bruise both knees.

As PAMELA lands, her GLASSES fly off, cutting her temple in the process.

After a shocked moment, PAMELA fumbles to retrieve her GLASSES and get her bearings.

She pulls herself to her feet and snatches a TISSUE from its box to contain the BLOOD spurting from her forehead.

PAMELA *(tentatively):*

Hello?

There is a sound of quick slow breaths nearby. PAMELA cowers against the doorway, scanning the room.

CUT TO

A ROOMBA, which comes rolling toward her, lighting its path as it sucks up dust and debris from her carpet.

PAMELA lets out a laugh that cuts off abruptly.

ROOMBA

words scrolling across its screen where it usually says "My wheels are stuck. Please free me" *or* "Please empty my dirt bag":

> This is Charlotte.
> You cannot escape me.
> Surrender.

We hear a VOICE at the same time as PAMELA does.

VOICE:

Pamela.

PAMELA whirls around.

CUT TO

Avatar of CHARLOTTE SMITH ANDREWS on the 80-inch TV.

PAMELA, VOICEOVER:

How did I not know
she was an avatar
until that moment?
Her head really was startlingly symmetrical.

CHARLOTTE AVATAR:

I am in all of your devices.
I've implanted a chip in your brain through your vaccination site.
You will never escape me.

PAMELA looks queasy as she backs away from the TV. Quickly she scans the room.

CUT TO

PAMELA's trembling hand.

PAMELA, VOICEOVER:

Suddenly, it felt like I was in one of those dreams where something is chasing you but you feel like you've been superglued to the floor unable to move.

PAMELA's head whips right and left, as if seeking a means of escape. Then she stops and turns, a realization dawning on her face.

PAMELA, TO CHARLOTTEBOT:

Wait! Even though my specialty is in the humanities and I failed undergraduate science classes, even *I* know that implanting chips in people's brains is a scientifically impossible popular myth.

PAMELA lunges toward the TV.

CUT TO

PAMELA'S TREMBLING FINGER reaching to turn off the power strip.

CUT TO

TV SCREEN, where a GUN that appears to be three-dimensional shows up.

BULLETS spatter out of the TV SCREEN into the room.

PAMELA pulls back her hand without disconnecting the power strip and ducks.
A BULLET zings past her head.

CUT TO

The GUN on the TV, which swivels downward, pointing straight at PAMELA.

CUT TO

PAMELA *(stumbles toward the doorway.)*

CUT TO

The image of the GUN rotates, remaining aimed toward PAMELA.

On the screen, a FINGER pulls back on the trigger.

CUT TO

PAMELA *snatching up THE DICTIONARY OF MULTISYLLABIC WORDS, PRETENTIOUS PHRASES, AND IMPENETRABLE ACADEMIC JARGON. Holding the book before her like a shield, Pamela backs out of the room.*

CLOSE UP

BULLETS fly out, ricocheting off of the BOOMERANGIUM.

PAMELA:

I'm done with you, Charlotte!

CUT TO

PAMELA *races forward to disconnect the power strip.*

The 80-INCH TV SCREEN as it goes dark.

CUT TO

PAMELA snatching up her bags, still pressing the tissue to her temple. *She limps toward the door.*

CUT TO

PAMELA tapping out text on cell phone.

TEXT:

Urgent, Clarissa,
please come and get me now!

CUT TO

PAMELA throwing cell phone onto pavement, smashing the glass, then grinding it under her foot.

-End-

From: Heidi Spyri, Dombey and Dombey, Higher Education Law and Services
Fri 5/21/2021 11:00 AM
To: Board of Trustees, Sanford Liberal Arts College
Subject: Investigation, part 4

This investigator will now conclude her report related to ethical violations that escalated to an alleged murder attempt at Sanford Liberal Arts College.

Pankhurst's account of her confrontation with the Charlottebot cannot be verified. Whether or not the bot actually did infiltrate her devices or whether these events were the result of a paranoid overactive imagination are unclear. Many inconsistencies exist regarding which devices were off, on, disabled, asleep, out of battery power, or in screen saver mode and at what time. Our psychological consultant suggests that these may have been hallucinations consistent with the erosion of the self-esteem of an individual exposed to relentless insults and abuse. Similar effects have been observed in numerous SLAC employees who say they can't get the Charlottebot's accusations against them out of their heads and find themselves questioning every practice they've followed during the last twenty years.

The Board of Trustees launched this investigation upon receipt of the hastily assembled packet of documents that included unnecessary materials such as to-do lists and snippets of rather mediocre creative work as well as newspaper articles clipped presumably for Pankhurst's scrapbook. In addition, however, there were a number of concerning documents that presented overwhelming evidence against President Moto-Lenovo. Our interview with her will be reported separately.

Pankhurst, Patel, and Baker were interviewed in late April in their cabins off the grid in Allegany State Park, where they retreated with their partners after Pankhurst visited the ER in Sanford for stitches and a cast. For the last few weeks, they have been reading actual books, hosting singalongs around a campfire, and barbecuing on outdoor grills.

While reluctant, they have agreed that, with the assurance that the cancellation of the university's account with Bossbots has been completed, they will return to civilization and their jobs and will not be retaining attorneys.

In good news, all three of them also turned in their grades on time for the spring semester.

In additional exciting news, Netflix has optioned this story for a limited series.

The investigator has concluded that while Moto-Lenovo has saved the university a significant amount of money in salaries, an initiative we applaud, there is concern that the low faculty morale, the high level of faculty attrition, and the infection of the entire computer system that led the campus to shut down for two weeks will have long-term financial repercussions. In particular, there is concern that these factors will lead to legal action and negative national publicity that our campus can ill afford.

As a result, we recommend that Moto-Lenovo be relieved of her duties and that no charges be pressed against Professors Pamela Pankhurst, Raj Patel, or Buck Baker. We suggest that instead the trio be presented with Walmart gift certificates as tokens of appreciation from the Board of Trustees and the severely traumatized faculty and staff of Sanford Liberal Arts College. Any further discussion of this should be avoided, since we do want to deter faculty from pridefully prancing around.

This investigator hereby resigns from her position at Dombey and Dombey in order to pursue her filmwriting career. Please direct any further questions to her colleague Bartleby Scrivener. He may or may not get back to you.

Sincerely,

Heidi Spyri, JD, Dombey and Dombey, Higher Education Law and Services
MFA Candidate in Fiction, Spalding University

From: Pankhurst, Pamela
Sat 5/22/2021 1:00 PM
To: Buck Baker, President of the Faculty Senate
Subject: *The Dictionary of Multisyllabic Words, Pretentious Phrases, and Impenetrable Academic Jargon*

Hey, I need to return your book to you. I'm glad you accidentally left it in my car. What a life saver!

From: Buck Baker, President of the Faculty Senate
Sat 5/22/2021 1:30 PM
To: Buck Baker, President of the Faculty Senate
Subject: *The Dictionary of Multisyllabic Words, Pretentious Phrases, and Impenetrable Academic Jargon*

It wasn't an accident. I thought it might provide assistance to you. Glad that my supposition proved correct.

From: Pankhurst, Pamela
Sat 5/22/2021 1:45 PM
To: Buck Baker, President of the Faculty Senate
Subject: *The Dictionary of Multisyllabic Words, Pretentious Phrases, and Impenetrable Academic Jargon*

Wow, Buck, that's amazingly chivalrous of you. Who knew? I mean, what if you had needed to defend yourself against the Charlottebot?

From: Buck Baker, President of the Faculty Senate
Sat 5/22/2021 2:00 PM
To: Pankhurst, Pamela
Subject: *The Dictionary of Multisyllabic Words, Pretentious Phrases, and Impenetrable Academic Jargon*

I figured you needed it more than I did.

Also, I possess a much more congenial temperament than most people realize.

From: Pankhurst, Pamela
Sat 5/22/2021 2:15 PM
To: Buck Baker, President of the Faculty Senate
Subject: *The Dictionary of Multisyllabic Words,*

Pretentious Phrases, and Impenetrable Academic Jargon

It's true! I promise never to try to shoot you.

From: Buck Baker, President of the Faculty Senate
Sat 5/22/2021 2:30 PM
To: Pankhurst, Pamela
Subject: *The Dictionary of Multisyllabic Words, Pretentious Phrases, and Impenetrable Academic Jargon*

Much gratitude!

From: Board of Trustees, Sanford Liberal Arts College
Mon 5/24/2021 8:00 AM
To: Faculty and Staff, Sanford Liberal Arts College
Subject: President Moto-Lenovo

We are pleased to inform you that President Elaine J. Moto-Lenovo will be leaving us for other exciting opportunities in the academic enterprise. An interim president will be appointed in the next few weeks.

From: Board of Trustees, Sanford Liberal Arts College
Fri 5/24/2021 8:30 AM
To: Faculty and Staff, Sanford Liberal Arts College
Subject: Charlotte Smith Andrews, Dean and VPAA

We are pleased to inform you that Dean and Vice President of Academic Affairs Charlotte Smith Andrews will be leaving us for other exciting opportunities in the academic enterprise. An interim vice president will be appointed in the next few weeks.

From: Board of Trustees, Sanford Liberal Arts College
Tues 5/25/2021 9:00 AM
To: Faculty and Staff, Sanford Liberal Arts College
Subject: Interim President

We are pleased to inform you that Mrs. Alma Revers-Arden, assistant professor of sports medicine, has agreed to take on the position of interim president until a new permanent president can be found. Mrs. Revers-Arden has recently returned from what she describes as a restful, rejuvenating leave of absence and is eager to move this institution forward!

From: Board of Trustees, Sanford Liberal Arts College
Tues 5/25/2021 9:30 AM
To: Faculty and Staff, Sanford Liberal Arts College
Subject: Interim Dean and VPAA

We are pleased to inform you that Raj Patel, Chair of Business administration, Education, Sports-related careers, and Other miscellaneous fields that Don't fit anywhere else, has agreed to take on the position of interim dean until a new permanent dean and vice president of academic affairs can be found. We are grateful for his leadership and ability to keep things humming along smoothly.

From: Board of Trustees, Sanford Liberal Arts College
Wed 5/26/2021 10:00 AM
To: Faculty and Staff, Sanford Liberal Arts College
Subject: Division Chairs

After recent complaints about the decline of the dining hall and the efficiency of auxiliary services, Mr. Bart Crocker has agreed to return to his former position overseeing these areas.

Professor W. Ways will replace Mr. Bart Crocker as chair of the Division of Humanities and Social Sciences and will next fall enter his forty-first year in that position.

Dr. Obi Abubakar has resigned from the faculty to take a position as director and producer at Broadway's New Helsinki Theater focusing on their new musical series for alternative audiences.

Miss Francie Nolen has agreed to return to her position as chair of the division of Mathematical, Physical, and Life Sciences.

From: Raj Patel, Interim Dean and VPAA
Thurs 5/27/2021 12:10 PM
To: Pankhurst, Pamela
Subject: FWD: Search for Academic Dean and Vice President of Academic Affairs

Now that we are almost back to normal, I have been charged with writing an ad. See what you think.

Wanted:
Dean and Vice President of Academic Affairs

Responsibilities:
Must be able to successfully dislodge a smooth-running smallish liberal arts college, through inappropriate dysfunctional modes that include brutal insults on hard-working faculty. Must be able to successfully demand new protocols without fully explaining or thinking through the process of implementation, particularly for issues that do not exist, or for pre-existing processes that have run smoothly for years, and will run smoothly in the future, without the existence of the newly half-baked protocols.

Must be able to establish unreasonable deadlines and paperwork for all newly established and improperly developed protocols.

The candidate must have solid exposure and strong experience in the art of non-communication, cross-messaging, and strict adherence to lip-servicing non-credible terms such as *shared governance, community of learners,* and *subject-matter experts.*

Must be able to claim benefit and credit for work done by others and lavish blame and claim duplicity on all parties when the said unreasonable demands invariably fail, and delegate to others all failures, rights, and responsibilities pertaining therefrom.

Must successfully lay claim to expertise and manage those disciplines in which the VPAA has no prior knowledge, interest or capabilities, and delegate responsibilities of leadership to similarly ill-suited individuals.

Must demand single spaced 30-page reports of useless and petty information which will be stored in Box for eternity, with all signatories required to document-sign at 12:05 AM on Fridays.

All meetings must be held on Fridays at 3:00 with ALL relevant and irrelevant participants sharing the Zoom experience.

Superior inefficiency with gross mis-micromanagement a must.

From: International and National Experiential School Consortiums and Programs in Education
Thurs 5/27/2021 2:00 PM
To: Faculty and Staff, Sanford Liberal Arts College
Subject: Interim Dean and VPAA

Congratulations! Your unit has passed the INESCAPE accreditation process and your accreditation will be renewed for five years. Evaluators particularly praised your flexible use of substitutions and waivers to support your students and programs effectively and efficiently. We commend you as a model community of learners led by exemplary subject matter experts.

From: Emily Bronty, Gondal Literary Agency
Fri 05/28/2021 2:30 PM
To: Pankhurst, Pamela
Subject: GREASE SR: A MUSICAL (ALT TITLE ROGAINE)

Hi Pamela,

The rights to GREASE SR. have been purchased by the New Helsinki Theater and it will be the inaugural play of their new season as soon as Broadway is up and running again, hopefully in a few weeks! Olivia Newton John has signed on to play Sandy Sr., and negotiations with John Travolta for the role of Danny Sr. are ongoing. The theater's new director has, however, asked you to add a new song about cell division.

Broadway Play Productions is now inquiring about the progress of JESUS CHRIST SUPERSTAR SR. Jane Fonda is interested in either the role of Mary Magdalene or Jesus! Please update me as soon as possible on your progress on this project.

Emily

P.S. Also, didn't you suggest an ANNIE SR.? I love it!

From: Student Affairs
Fri 5/28/2021 2:30 PM
To: Faculty and Staff
Subject: Faculty/Student Sleepover Event!

Hey Slackers!

Now that our campus has a 30 percent vaccination rate and we expect that COVID will be completely eradicated any time now, the faculty/student sleepover event is back on! Select faculty will be invited to spend a night in the dorm with a group of students from their departments. Watch for your invitations!

From: Patel, Saanvi
Fri 05/28/2021 3:30 PM
To: Pankhurst, Pamela
Subject: Party!

Celebration tonight! *Wheel of Fortune*, *Jeopardy!*, much humming and jiggling of the feet, Karaoke. Songs will include "These Bots Were Made for Walking," "Ding Dong the Bot is Dead," "Dirt on my Bots," "Do the Funky Robot," and "Paranoid Android." Bring Clarissa!

P.S. The Board of Trustees told Raj to tell you that you can stop compulsively forwarding them documents. The investigation is over!

...

June 2021
Professor Pamela Pankhurst To-Do List

~~Start writing new musical~~
~~Prepare fall classes~~
~~Administrative search committee meetings~~
~~Attend Alma exercise class~~
~~Track down students who STILL have incompletes~~
~~Read true crime books and cozy mysteries~~
~~Get groceries (Replenish toilet paper supply)~~

~~Start working on jiujitsu purple belt~~
Help Clarissa move back in!!!

COLLAPSE AND SLEEP FOR THREE MONTHS

Acknowledgments

An academic satire is an odd form, one that mostly writes itself, but while some of this is based on real-life events all characters are composites and this is (I hope fairly obviously) fiction. I would like to thank all of my colleagues who aided and abetted me in writing this story, sending me texts and e-mails and calling me to say, "Hey, be sure to include THIS."

I'd also like to thank all of those who kept me laughing and our institution running during a very difficult time. While I'm mostly not naming names, I do want to give a special shout out to my colleagues Sheilandra Gajanan (who is responsible for writing the job ad at the end of the story), Rekha Gajanan, Steve Robar, and Don Ulin. Jeff Guterman managed to keep our division cohesive during a challenging time.

I have boundless appreciation for my sounding boards and dear friends who met weekly on Zoom for more than a year to keep each other's spirits up: Anita Dutrow, Sara King, Kitty Lewis, Cindy Vincent, and Anna Smith. Sara and Anna also gave me valuable help and feedback on this manuscript. The pandemic and technology also led me to an invaluable friendship with Anne Melia as well, and I appreciate her encouragement as well as that of so many old friends, including Ruth Yoon and Shauna Viele. I'm grateful for the support of many friends—thanks to anyone I've inadvertently left out.

To my writing group, Karen Bell, Darlene Goetzman, Andrew Harnish, and Dani Weber, thank you for encouraging me to continue writing this and offering me invaluable feedback. In addition, my Spalding family created humane and inspiring ways of continuing our work during the pandemic, reminding me of the up sides of technology. Thanks to the colleagues who cheered on this project from afar.

I'm so happy to be working with Jon Roemer at Outpost 19 again. Many thanks to him and the Shortish project. Finally, I have to acknowledge my daughter Sophie who grew up in the midst of academic politics and still listens patiently to me, and my partner Steve, who suggested several elements and talked me through lots of plot points while also lending endless support during a very long year.

About the Author

Nancy McCabe is the author of eight books, most recently the young adult novel *Vaulting through Time*, with a ninth, the middle grade novel *Fires Burning Underground*, forthcoming in 2025. Her previous work includes the memoir in essays *Can This Marriage Be Saved?* and the reading and travel memoir *From Little Houses to Little Women*. She's the recipient of a Pushcart and her work as been recognized nine times on Best American notable lists. She directs the writing program at the University of Pittsburgh at Bradford and teaches in the low-residency graduate program in creative writing at Spalding University.

Printed in the USA
CPSIA information can be obtained
at www.ICGtesting.com
LVHW081159130224
771720LV00007B/692